THE TERROR OF DUNWALL

MIKE D MARTIN

THE TERROR OF DUNWALL

The Knight from Kildwin
Book 1

A part of the Elesian Tale Saga

This book is a work of fiction. Names, characters, places, and incidents are the product of the author's imagination or are used fictitiously. Any resemblance to actual events, locales, or persons, living or dead, is coincidental.

Copyright © 2021 by Mike Martin

All rights reserved.

No part of this book may be reproduced in any form or by any electronic or mechanical means, including information storage and retrieval systems, without written permission from the author, except for the use of brief quotations in a book review.

ISBN (e-book): 978-1-7379960-3-3

ISBN (Paperback): 978-1-7379960-2-6

Edited by Jen Salzer

Cover Art by Andrei Bat.

Check out Andrei's work at: http://99designs.com/profiles/bandrei

CHAPTER 1

With each heavy step of the horse's mighty foot Marcus felt himself growing ever more nervous. He tried to calm himself. He took short deep breaths and tried to prepare himself for what was about to happen. When his eyes were closed, he was at ease. But as soon as they opened and he looked at the three men clopping along around him, the feelings of fear and nausea washed over him again as quickly as it disappeared when he closed his eyes.

The man to his left, a man named Piers glanced over at him. When their eyes met the man looked concerned for only a brief moment before a smirk parted his lips. Marcus thought of telling the man he did not appreciate the smirk but quickly bit his tongue. The man was the highest ranking knight aside from their commander. A weathered man with skin that looked more leather than flesh due to the countless days he spent with the sweltering sun beating down upon him, Piers was the man responsible for training every man and woman brought to the Knights of the King with a blade. He was a man who was somehow both adored by his students and feared by them. They once said that he had never been bested with a blade and that the only man who had ever come close to beating him was Castron.

But they said that no longer. Not after what had happened last week. On that morning Piers, the mighty sword master who had been swinging blades around each morn to teach the young and inexperienced knights for over fifty years, had been disarmed and bested by Marcus, a man of only 22 summers. Worse still was that Marcus only had 10 years of blade training beneath his belt. The others he trained with and the other knights had all gathered around the first time their blades had crossed. Not one of them seemed to believe their eyes when the nicked and worn blade of Piers was knocked from his grip by a ferociously quick strike from Marcus that the man had not seemed to see coming. It had impressed everyone watching the commotion.

Even Castron, their commander, a man who had told them upon their arrival to the fortress that he would not even bother to learn their names until they proved to him that their names were worth knowing, had seemed impressed. Marcus had assumed it was only surprise and nothing more. But as he would quickly find out that he was wrong.

The next morning at training Piers had sent the others to spar and taken Marcus into the main fortress, a place where only those who had completed their first hunt and killed their first beast and become true Knights of the King were allowed to enter. He hadn't even had the time to take in the grandeur of it. The white tile floors and stone columns in the main room made the small wooden barrack that he'd spent the past 10 years living in seem nearly uninhabitable. The stairs, the walls, even the ceiling seemed to glow. It seemed a palace fit for royalty, not men who hunted monsters. Yet, this was their home. And it would be their home until the end of days.

Piers had led him up more stairs than he'd ever seen in all his days and when it seemed he'd climbed more stairs than any man should have ever had to climb they'd gone up more. At the top of the stairs he found himself within the walls of Castron's study, the brutish old man carefully studying maps and rolls of parchment when the two of them had arrived. The commander had risen from his chair and his heart had caught in his throat. It was well known amongst all those training with the Knights of the King that if you saw a neatly trimmed beard of white speckled with black flakes and a shaggy white mane of a fearsome lion approaching, you'd best start praying. Because Commander Castron was coming to see you. And if the man didn't slap you stupid for making a mistake, then the man was coming to give you such a vicious tongue lashing that you'd still hear the words rattling in your mind while you were trying to sleep a week later.

But Castron had done neither thing that day. Instead, he'd asked him if he was ready to be a Knight of the King. He'd lied, of course, and told the man that he was. Many nights when he lay down to sleep he thought of sneaking off and leaving in the middle of the night. They'd not miss one man. He could go off and live whatever life he wanted, not subservient to the line of the kings whose name was Sylvian. He would not have to hunt down strange beasts and slaughter men and creature alike. He could know peace.

Yet whenever the ugly thought reared itself within his head, he convinced himself that his father, the bastard that he was, had been right when he dropped him at the fortress all those years ago with only a sword his grandfather had won in a game of cards. His father had told him that he belonged there. And almost as soon as he started training with the others, as soon as he started progressing to be more skilled than any of the other recruits, he began to think his father had been right. This was where he was meant to be. He just didn't understand why.

So he'd agreed to undergo whatever test it was that Castron had in mind if it meant he would become a Knight of the King.

The commander had handed Marcus the only possession he had left of his old life. It was taken by the commander the day his father had dropped him off and the old man had told him that the blade would return to its rightful owner the day he was ready to be a knight. It was an ancestral sword, the one his grandfather had won. Though he wasn't quite sure how one blade could be better than another, he had accepted it from his father then as he accepted it from Castron. Then Castron had told him that the next time someone came in need of their help, Marcus would ride out with his fellow knights or he would ride out alone to kill whatever needed killed. If he survived, he would be made a knight.

If he hadn't been nervous about it that morning, he was more than making up for it now. His stomach lurched as they rounded a corner on the small dirt path they followed and the smell of death met his nostrils. A foul smell carried on the air that seemed to grow stronger and more odorous with each heavy step the mare beneath him took. He looked to the area right around the path where the villagers of the town of Dunwall had cut the trees down to expand their town, but saw nothing. He turned his gaze out into the forest. But he could see nothing amongst the green back-drop of the trees.

Marcus grumbled under his breath and kept riding, following mindlessly along as the village chieftain of Dunwall, a short and pudgy man who never seemed to be without food and ale in his hands, led them back to his town. His eyes found their way to the bald chieftain as he nibbled gingerly at a large apple from the city of Concord and Marcus nearly shook his head in disgust. It was the chieftain's village that was under attack by some strange beast that was beyond his comprehension to even explain. It was his villagers who were dying and rebelling against him because of this strange beast. And it was he who had rode all the way to the fortress to beg Castron to personally tend to the beast for him.

Yet it was Marcus who was overcome with nerves while the chieftain munched jovially on the apple, laughing and offering jests to Commander Castron as he rode beside the man, though Marcus could tell his commander was not in good humor for he never laughed once. The old man's grunts and grumbles of annoy-ance could not have been clearer, even to Marcus as he brought up the rear of their group. But the oblivious man did not seem to notice. Or worse, he didn't care.

Marcus wanted to calm his nerves somehow so he turned his attention towards the forests around them as they snaked their way along the trail, slowly climbing up the side of a long gently sloping hillside which felt like more of a small mountain based upon how long it was taking them to get to the top. Dunwall lay on the other side of the hill, nestled at the base if the untrustworthy chieftain was to be believed. With each stride forward they drew a little closer to the town beset by some beast, and a little bit closer to the most important moments of Marcus' life.

The forests around him were still, unlike the thoughts and worries that raced across his mind as he pictured every monster and beast he'd ever learned about. Goblins, trolls, banshees, vampires, werewolves. All of them and more flashed across his brain like a jolt of lightning before they quickly receded to be replaced by another. He thought of every scenario he'd ever been taught, of the weak points that he was to exploit, of the flanking maneuvers and oils of plants that would drive beasts into frenzies when the smell met their noses. He thought of everything. And it only made him more nervous.

The forest didn't help either. The stillness made him think more. His hometown, the place where he'd lost his mother and where the father who abandoned him still lived was bordered by a dense forest to the south and he'd never seen that forest as calm as this one. No matter the time of day, he'd always seen things moving around in the trees. And that he saw nothing here only raised more questions. Did the animals of the forest know of the beast plaguing these lands and strive to avoid it? Had the beast driven the animals away or worse, killed them all? Or was there something else happening here, something too strange for him to be able to guess?

Marcus grumbled and shook his head in frustration. He'd hoped the forest would calm the raging fire of nervousness in his mind. But all he had successfully done was feed the flames and turn them into a towering inferno that was shifting and changing into something both different and somehow the same. Nervousness gave way to curiosity and fear. A cold chill crawled up his spine like a spider, causing his entire body to shiver in the midday sun.

Then, a shadow passed by overhead. The young man turned his gaze heavenward, his eyes searching for the beast that had produced the shadow that had fallen over him for a brief moment. He only caught a brief glimpse of the creature, but he was certain it had been one of the greater drakes of the world, a lesser dragon. A wyvern perhaps. It was only in his view for a brief moment before it dove into the forests, the beast disappearing from his view before he could get a good look at it. He wasn't sure what it was if he was being honest. It might have been a wyvern or it could have been something else entirely. But he began to ponder if maybe the beast they hunted was in fact a wyvern and he tried to recall everything he'd ever been taught about drakes and dragons.

He'd been so consumed by his thoughts he hadn't noticed Commander Castron falling back until his horse was cantering along beside his, keeping stride with him. It was only when his commander had loudly cleared his throat that Marcus cast a glance in his commander's direction. As soon as he saw the man beside him, he bowed his head respectfully.

"You seem quiet. More quiet than most do on such journeys," the commander noted after a short pause. There was another much longer pause as the man seemed to contemplate what words he should say next. "I remember on my testing day, as I rode to kill a pack of goblins that had beset a small town near the coast called Guffin, I nearly turned around. And when I arrived, I could barely speak a word to any in the town. It was like my breath had caught in my throat and refused to release. So being nervous and quiet, I understand. But you've not said a word since we left the fortress."

Marcus nodded his head in agreement, carefully choosing the next words that he would say to the man who, if all things went well, would be the man he answered to for a great many moons. "I've been thinking."

Castron grumbled as he swatted at a fly that had taken to buzzing around his sweat laden head. "What thoughts plague your mind?"

Marcus found his free hand make its way to the handle of his sword, the only reminder of the boy he had been before he had begun his training to become the man that he was now. He tapped the pommel of his blade nervously, though if the commander saw, he did not say. "A simpler question would be what doesn't," he answered his commander with a shrug. "I think of the things you've taught us. I look for signs in the forests."

When he turned to face the commander, he saw that a small smile had crinkled the corner of his mouth. But the old man, prideful as he was, allowed his face to become stoic again as soon as he noticed Marcus's gaze. "And what have you seen in the woods?"

"Nothing." He shook his head. "It's as if the forests have been stilled to silence. Animals or beasts, seems to matter not. There is nothing happening in the trees. No clues there."

"Are there really no clues to be found?" the old man asked him carefully. "Perhaps the silencing of the trees and the animals within the forests are the clues which we should take heed of." He cast his eyes to the trees for a brief moment, watching as an abnormally calm forest met his eyes, before he turned back to Marcus and asked "What manner of beast or monster will cause animals to flee the forests?"

"None that fit the description the chieftain gave us." His answer drew a look of intrigue from his commander so he quickly continued, hoping his rationale would be met with agreement from the old man. "Werewolves can. But they're not abnormally tall and able to be lost amongst the trees. The same can be said about those afflicted with the Cannibal's curse. Wendigo are monstrous, territorial. They'll drive away even the most lethal of animals. But again... they're not large enough." He opened his mouth to say something about the wyvern he thought that he'd seen but thought better of it. If they hadn't seen the shadow pass overhead, perhaps the beast hadn't been a wyvern after all. And he did not want to seem foolish in front of his future commander.

"Does the same go for Selvans and Nymphs?" Marcus turned to face his commander at the mention of such creatures. The old man had taught him that those creatures were either beasts lost to time or legends altogether. At first, all he felt was confusion.

But it quickly gave way to understanding. Another test. Castron was trying to see how well he remembered their lessons.

"If they existed to begin with, yes." His answer drew another smile from Castron and this time the man did not try to hide it. "No need to concern ourselves with those."

"I would have to agree," the old man said kindly. He motioned with his head towards the chieftain as he rode ahead of them, eating something else which Marcus could not make out from the distance. "But our dear friend did tell me that the people here speak of a local legend, a monster of the forest which every 100 years awakens from a deep slumber in the heart of the forest to feed before it retreats to slumber once more. They call him 'The Horned One'. But I believe that he speaks of an Old God called 'Hernos the Horned One'. An Old God who was revered as the King of the Forests."

Marcus nearly scoffed at the idea but thought better of it given his present company. Castron was a man of faith. He believed in the Creator, prayed to the God of Light and all creation each morning and each night. But Marcus, the scorned man that he was, had little faith since the day the Creator saw fit to steal his mother from him and leave him with a father who had never wanted the boy to begin with. With each passing day that faith seemed to grow ever fainter, the old prayers he offered to a deaf eared god little more than distant memory he could hardly remember anymore.

So he held his tongue for the commander's benefit. "Are we to believe that these men ask us here to kill a beast that they once revered as a god?"

The old man shook his head. "According to their legends, Hernos would have awoken 60 summers past. He's not to awaken for another 40. And if the legends of the Old Gods are to be believed... Then there is no way that Hernos the Horned Once can be the beast which is plaguing these woods."

"But what if it is Hernos," Marcus suggested somewhat bashfully. When the old man craned his neck with a confused look upon his face he regretted even opening his mouth to begin with.

But it was too late to take the words back now. All he could do now was say what he was thinking and hope the man wouldn't find him a fool. "Perhaps this 'horned one' they speak of is not an Old God at all. Perhaps it never was and the creature which they call Hernos is merely another beast which they have mistaken for the Old God of legend."

Castron thought for a moment and then smiled. "You've a sharp mind, boy. Nearly as sharp as the blade you wear around your waist. If your hand wields that blade like the man whose hands once wielded it, you may yet be the best among us."

Marcus gave the man an appreciative nod and watched as Castron spurred his horse forward, rejoining the chieftain as they neared the crest of the hill. Marcus followed after the men as his mind began to race once more, though not about the monsters and beasts of the lands. Instead his mind began to think of the sword that hung from his waist. The sword of a legendary Knight of the King known by many names; The Dragon Slayer, The Pact Maker, The Oath Keeper and to some who believed in such nonsense, The Grave Walker. But to Marcus and the other Knights of the King, the man was known by only one name. Artorigus.

Artorigus had been the greatest Knight of the King. He had been a knight in days which were long past in the lands of Elesia, a kingdom with short memory. The true years of his service lost to all but memory and stories. All they knew was that he had been one of the last men to serve the Knights of the King when their numbers were held to five. According to Castron it was after Artorigus that the knights had begun recruiting men in greater numbers and the old man claimed to be one of the early men to join as their numbers swelled to dozens. Whether it was true or not, Marcus did not know. Men had a tendency to lie as much as history and legends did.

But he did know a few things to be truths about the legendary knight called Artorigus. He knew that the man had fought in the Great Dragon Wars against his will. And upon the top of Fereldon Hill, the place of the last great battle between man and dragon. Dragons were the hardest beasts to kill in all the known world, their large scales near impervious to the attacks of man and their fiery breath a destructive force of nature that could reduce the strongest building to rubble in the blink of an eye. Yet Artorigus had killed three that day.

The only problem was that the man did not find his feat worth celebrating. He found no glory or honor in doing battle with the oldest and wisest of creatures. He knew both man and dragon possessed the same crippling weakness as one another, pride. So in the aftermath of the battle, the knight had snuck away in defiance of the king and found his way to the only surviving male dragon, the son of the Lord of the Dragons. Artorigus had met with the dragon knowing he would likely die, given that it had been Artorigus who had killed the last male's father. The knight had killed the Lord of the Dragons, and still he went to meet with the dragon's son.

The last male, a dragon with scales of glittering gold, was not fond to see the man who killed his father before him. But when the two began to speak, they came to an understanding. They had both agreed that the Great Dragon Wars needed to end before the last of his kind were killed off or man was driven to the brink of extinction.

In secret Artorigus and the Golden Dragon had flown into the heart of a great volcano. It was there that the dragon fashioned a legendary sword which he adorned with the broken scales that had once covered his father's body. Upon the passing of the sword from dragon to man, a pact was made. A pact which ensured the end of man's hunting of the beasts and the end of dragons over-populating the lands, though few knew what was truly agreed upon with the fires of the volcano between man and dragon.

To this day ,the pact had remained unbroken. The only things which remained of the Pact was the memory of what Artorigus had told the king when he stood before the man to explain why he'd committed treason and the blade that he had carried until the day he had died. A blade that would be lost upon Artorigus' death, only for the grandfather of Marcus, a man whose name or face he could not recall, to win it in a game of cards. So the sword of legend, the Dragon Pact Sword, dangled from the waist of a man who was not yet a Knight of the King. A man who would not become a knight if he could not figure out what manner of beast lurked in these woods and kill it. Or if it killed him.

He would not be the first Knight of the King to be killed by a beast he was hunting. He would not be the last if it did. People didn't die in their beds in Elesia. Even Artorigus, for all his strength and cunning, had been killed while hunting for a beast of darkness unlike any these lands had seen since. The legends claimed that he laid down his life so the other knights could escape. It was only by his sacrifice that the others were able to cut the beast down.

Only myth and legend did not allow the man to stay dead. There existed a myth that when the world found itself in great danger when the Destroyer, the ancient God of Darkness and Destruction, escaped from his eternal prison and began to lay waste to the world, Artorigus, blessed by the Creator's light, had arisen from the dead. The knight had taken up his old sword and armor and led men into battle against the ancient Lord of Darkness at the Sanctuary, a holy place where those who wished could offer prayers to the Creator at the spot where it was believed he had departed for the heavens. Artorigus had defeated the Destroyer that day and had earned a new moniker. He became known as Artorigus the Grave Walker, the man who returned from the Halls of His Fathers to save the world of man once more.

A story Marcus knew to be a lie. No man could cheat death. There was a finality to dying, an ending to the first path of life. He was certain of that. Artorigus had not returned from the dead that day. No matter what the people claimed.

Marcus shook his head and tried to brush the legends of Artorigus from his mind, though his hand still tapped nervously on the pommel of the legendary knight's sword as he tried to focus on his own coming battles and not upon the battles of a man long dead.

He glanced forward and was surprised when he saw that the other three in his company had stopped upon the crest of the hill. He spurred his horse onward and she raced up the last stretch of incline.

The hill sloped sharply downward, a narrow path that zigzagged along the hill in long sweeping curves led down into the valley. In the center of the valley the small town of Dunwall stood, a town of wooden buildings with thatched roofs that looked to be in a state of disrepair. Marcus found himself unable to pay much mind to the actual buildings. Instead, his eyes were focused on the area around the outside of the town where it appeared the villagers had been clearing the forests that surrounded them on all side. The stumps of dozens of trees around the perimeter of the village were visible from where they sat on the hilltop.

He cast a sideways glance at Piers and then at Castron. When both men greeted his gaze with the same look, he suspected that they were having the same thoughts as him. In ancient times it was said that if man tried to clear the forests, the forests would fight back. It was why they claimed that Direwood Forest, the most dangerous forest in all the lands, was the riskiest endeavor that man had ever willingly undertaken. Thousands of men had perished to cut down those evil haunted woods and drive the monsters from within so the king could build his castle upon those lands. Marcus suspected that this was no different. These people had been cutting down the trees and clearing the forests for their own gain. And the forests had fought back. Somehow, someway, the forest had sent a beast to kill those responsible for its destruction.

Castron cleared his throat loudly and the old man turned towards the chieftain. The commander slicked a river of sweat from his forehead and rubbed his hand through his hair, matting the white mane atop his head. "When did this beast appear?"

"Few weeks ago maybe," the chieftain answered, though the flippant and callous nature with which he said it told Marcus that he did not truly know. Or he did not care.

Castron must have sensed it to, for his angered grunt was

nearly as mocking as the words he spoke next. "They say a man's memory is only as long as the days that pass between each drink of ale. By my guess your memory is no longer than half a day." The man opened his mouth to offer protest but thought better of it as soon as he saw the glare on Castron's face, a menacing glare which would have even frightened the Destroyer himself into submission gracing the weathered and wrinkled face of the old man.

"Can you at least tell us when your people began cutting the trees down?" Piers asked before their commander could in his typical biting and yet, somehow blunt tone. "Or have you also drunk away that memory?"

Again, the chieftain looked poised to lash out with his tongue. But once more he bit his lip and grumbled a few words under his breath. The man seemed intent to not answer. But when he caught sight of the glare the two knights were giving him he sighed reluctantly. "I cannot remember. All I know is that the presence of the beast and the destruction of the forest began near to one another. Days apart, perhaps? Maybe more? I can't... I don't remember."

"Then I suggest you point us in the direction of someone who can remember," Castron said. Marcus could hear an edge to his voice, as sharp as freshly made steel. It was the voice that made those training under the Knights of the King pray when they saw the man coming. Grating and sharp as a dagger, that tone could cut even the biggest of men to nothing.

The four men sat astride their horses in silence after that, waiting for the chieftain to regain his wits and lead them back to the small town which he supposedly ruled over. But the portly man with a misshapen nose and crooked smile merely continued indulging in his food and drinks with an almost wanton disregard for his village below.

Castron seemed to have grown impatient though it was Piers who looked ready to pounce on the man for his indifference. The sword master's weathered face hardened. His hand grasped for the well worn handle of his blade. But their commander gave him a stern grunt and Piers' hand fell lax. "I suggest you get your steed moving or my men will return to the fortress and you will be left at the mercy of your beast," Castron threatened.

"You'd not leave us at the mercy of The Horned One," the chieftain cried in defiance, seemingly trying to call Castron's bluff. A mistake if Marcus had ever seen one.

"I'd leave you at the mercy of a banshee before I'd help a man who doesn't seem to care for his people," was Castron's menacing reply. "Either lead us to the village and point us to one who can remember what has happened or we leave." The chieftain stumbled upon his words and succeeded in saying nothing. He whined and protested something that Marcus did not hear, though he did not hear because he did not want to.

But Marcus did hear his commander give them a single stern order. Return to the fortress. The three men turned, Marcus doing so with great reluctance. They began to descend the hill. It had been a long, arduous ride. Marcus had been wracked with nervousness. His mind had raced and his sword arm had trembled nervously for the entire journey. And it had all been for nothing.

Or at least he thought it would all be for nothing until they heard the scream pierce the stillness of the forest around them. It had not been the scream of a banshee or troll or any other of the beasts which could shriek so loudly that the sound would carry on the air.

No. This had been the scream of a woman.

CHAPTER 2

"Where did that come from?" Castron asked sharply as soon as the scream faded to nothing and silence replaced it. He spun his horse about in circles, his eyes darting back and forth. He searched the forest around them but saw nothing. Marcus knew the forest was not where that scream had come from. And he suspected the old man knew it too. Finally he turned to Piers and then Marcus. He asked them the same question again. "Where did that come from?"

Marcus did not answer. Because they had to know already. It had come from the valley on the opposite side of the hill. It had been the scream of one of the villagers they'd just turned their backs on.

As the silence of the two men greeted him, the commander's face became solemn. His shoulder's sagged weakly and wordlessly he spun his horse around and galloped back up the hill. Marcus and Piers followed after him.

Marcus nearly grumbled with disgust when he saw that the chieftain, for all his talk of caring for his village, had still not moved from his place atop the crest of the hill. A part of him, the darkest and most primal part, wanted to draw the blade and slash it through the man's body. It would be a benefit to the villagers he'd so carelessly failed. The man deserved that fate. He deserved to die.

But Marcus did not draw the blade. The chieftain deserved to have his head cut free from his body or the sharp point of his sword driven through his chest. But just because he deserved to die did not mean that Marcus deserved the right to kill him. Castron and Piers had both warned them for many moons that just because someone deserved death did not give one the right to kill them. Knights only killed those that they needed to. They did not kill for personal gratification or because of emotion. They killed because they had no other choice.

Marcus galloped past the man without even acknowledging his existence, following closely behind Castron and Piers as their horses followed the winding zigzagging trail that led down the hillside. The mighty hooves of their horses thundered loudly on the dirt path, throwing up so much dust that Marcus could barely see the horse in front of him. On more than one occasion his horse had nearly run right off the trail and into one of the waiting trees. But he had been able to tug the mare's reins and get her back on the right path with relative ease. For that he was thankful.

But he was not thankful for the dust that lingered on the air around him. It was the price he paid for riding at the back of their small pack. It swirled all around him, spiraling up into his nose with each sharp breath he drew in, making him feel he needed to sneeze. It dried his lips. When he opened his mouth to let loose numerous sneezes the dust found its way inside. The taste of dirt was all he knew. In those brief moments as they thundered down the hill like charging stampeding beasts, he was afraid he'd taste the dirt until long after the flesh had rotted from his bones.

When the dirt trails upon the hill fell away and were replaced by trails of trampled grass made by the frequent walking of the villagers, he nearly breathed a sigh of relief.

They were getting close to the village now, though Marcus was hardly sure it could even be called that. He saw no stalls for men and women to sell food and drink. He saw no tavern or shops to buy armor and weapons. All he saw were a number of houses, a couple dozen by his guessing, arranged haphazardly around a large clearing in the forest which was slowly getting bigger thanks to the men removing the trees nearest the homes. There were no streets, no central square or gathering places of any sorts, just wooden homes and grass.

The three men bounded between the houses, following the trampled pathways of grass. They weaved around both houses and people alike as they quickly made their way towards the far side of the village. Marcus wasn't sure what he'd expected when they rode into the small village. Cheers of joy? Shouts of thanks? Something. Anything.

Instead, all they received were hateful glares as the villagers stepped out of the way of their horses as they moved quickly towards a slowly gathering crowd near the edge of the village. Castron barked at the people as they moved, telling them to move aside. But they did not heed his warnings until the horses were nearly upon them. Then once they'd jumped aside to avoid being trampled, they'd bark words that made Marcus want to return words more hateful and biting than the ones they'd used.

He wanted to ask the commander if they were truly well served in this place where the villagers seemed less than pleased to even see them. But he thought better of it. These people needed their help. It didn't matter how vile and rude they were to them. They were frightened, besieged by a beast that they believed to be an unstoppable Old God. They had every right to be untrusting of men claiming they could kill such a beast. But even so, he thought it foolish of them to dismiss them without even talking to them, no matter how scared and nervous they were.

Castron slowed his horse to a canter and Marcus followed his lead. The three men slowly approached the crowd of villagers and one by one they slowly turned to look at them. The villager's faces were fraught with grief and fear. Some of them kept casting weary glances over their shoulders like they expected this strange beast to emerge from the trees and kill them all where they stood. But the beast never came.

"Greetings," Castron said formally, placing his free hand on his chest and bowing respectfully from the back of his horse. "My name is Castron. I am the commander of the Knights of the King. We have ridden here at the behest of your chieftain to help you deal with the beast that plagues your village."

An old woman stepped from the crowd and approached Castron with slow labored steps aided by a thick walking stick. She was a small and frail looking woman, one who looked like a strong wind would carry her away if it caught hold of her. Her beady eyes danced between the three men. Marcus found his eyes focusing on the wrinkles and discolored patches of skin upon her face. They reminded him of a woman he'd known long ago when he was just a boy. She had been the one who had mended his wounds when he hurt himself playing with his friends Kan and Gerald. She'd been the kindest and gentlest woman he'd ever met, save for his mother.

But as soon as the old woman before them spoke, he quickly realized this woman was far from that kind woman. "You come to our village to help us when we did not ask for your help," the old woman said curtly. Her voice was cold, angry even and she had a bitterness about her that was unwelcoming. "And you return without our chieftain, I do see. Tell me, knight, did you kill him and leave him for the wolves? For that would have been the best service you could've done for our village."

Castron and Piers exchanged an uncomfortable glance. "Your chieftain isn't dead. We rode ahead when we heard the screams," Piers offered.

The old woman shook her head. "A pity."

"Where did that scream come from, m'lady?" Castron asked.

"From the forest, of course. A few of our own decided to venture into the forest to make an offering to The Horned One so that he may be appeased and leave us alone once more. But they've yet to return. It would appear that our God has not accepted our offering."

"Have you sent anyone into the forest to find them?" The old knight's words were heavy with worry.

The old woman shook her head. "The Horned One got them already. There's no need to venture into those woods in search of those that are already dead. We will continue on with our lives and hope that one day our God will accept the offerings we leave for him. And you, knight, will leave this place and leave us to deal with this matter on our own."

Castron's eyes narrowed to slits, his face half contorted into a snarl as he looked at the old woman before them. "Do you speak for the village or only for yourself?" he asked, trying to be as calm as he could be even though his tone was forceful and demanding.

"I speak for Dunwall," the old woman said. "And I have spoken." There was a finality to her words. Marcus expected Castron to offer protest to the woman. If Marcus felt the woman had overstepped her authority then surely the commander felt the same. But Castron allowed the woman to turn her back on them and rejoin the gathered crowd. "Back towards the forest, all of you," she ordered sternly. "We must offer prayers to the Horned One in hopes that we will be able to calm his wearied mind. This is the only way."

Marcus watched as a few of the villagers did as she commanded, turning around and facing the forest. But the rest remained staring back at the Knights of the King, their eyes pleading for help, though they did not open their mouths to ask for it. He wanted to speak to them, to try to reason with them. But it was not his place. He was not the commander of the knights, nor was he even a knight. Not yet, anyways.

"Come, they do not wish our help it seems," Castron said much louder than he normally spoke. "We make haste back to the fortress. There are others out there who do need our help." At first Marcus was confused why the man was nearly shouting his orders. But then, like a bucking bronco, it hit him. The commander, the wise old man that he was, had put the townspeople who looked ready to plead for help in a predicament. They could ask for their help now or they could live and die by the rulings of an old woman who, by all rights, did not have the power to do what she'd done.

No one said a word. Castron gave Piers a quick nod and the two knights spun their horses around and began to retreat through the village. But Marcus did not follow. He remained rooted to the spot, watching the villagers as their pleading eyes turned to desperation and fear. One of them had to say something. They had to.

Thankfully, one of them did.

"Wait!" The voice of a woman called out sharply and from the crowd a woman not much older than Marcus with a baby clutched tightly against her chest, emerged. She walked briskly towards him, and he turned to see that the knights were cantering back towards him, a smug smile upon Piers' face. Castron's trick had worked.

"The old woman does not speak for all of Dunwall," she said in desperation. Marcus found his eyes drawn past the woman and towards the older woman who was glaring at her with pure scorn and hate upon her brow. That made him smile. "She speaks only for herself and the old. The beast that plagues us in not something that can be prayed away. It does not seek offerings and gifts of our people. It seeks to kill us all. And kill it has. Many of us have lost friends and family... sons and daughters... husbands..." At that, the woman looked down at her baby as a tear stung at the corner of her eye. "We need help. We need the beast to die or we need it driven away. We cannot do so by ourselves. Please... help us."

Castron looked down at the woman from his horse and asked a question that Marcus knew was meant to mock the old woman. "Do you speak for Dunwall then m'lady?"

"Aye, I do," the woman said as a chorus of agreement rang out from behind her. "I speak for those in Dunwall who will not allow fear to rule us. I speak for those who remember the days of our youths when we could walk and play in these woods without fear of never returning home. If it is gold you require, we will gladly pay it. Just please... rid us of this terror."

Marcus watched the old woman with cautious eyes and without even realizing it he noticed his sword hand had found its way to the handle of the blade. He half expected her to protest the woman's claims. In the moment he wouldn't have been surprised at all if the woman offered retaliation. But to his surprise the old woman grunted in disgust and returned her attention to the forest, offering prayers to a beast which did not want or need them.

"We do not require gold m'lady," Castron's voice boomed. "We only come to aid you in any way that we can. Now, please, return to your homes and await our return. We do not yet know if our presence will anger this beast. If any should be caught outside, I cannot say if its wrath will make its way to the village."

At that the old woman turned and leveled her finger towards Castron. Her eyes were narrow slits, nostrils flared with anger. "If you anger the Horned One and bring its wrath down upon us..." she started saying accusatory.

Marcus had heard enough. Before the woman could make whatever threat she had intended to make, he sharply cut her off. "If we anger this beast, we can only pray that it sees fit to kill you first. And slowly so you may look upon your God in all his glory."

The old woman looked taken aback but he did not care. The words felt right as he'd said them. Marcus noticed that the smirk had returned to his commander's face. He beckoned them onward and got his horse moving towards the forest where the men had gone missing.

Marcus followed as Castron and Piers made their way past the crowd. The three men carefully avoided the raised stumps where trees had once stood. There must have been hundreds of stumps on this end of the village alone. That was too many trees. He felt a chill race down his back. The forest was fighting back.

The three of them rode in relative silence for a long while as they snaked and weaved their way through the dense underbrush of the forest. Occasionally Castron would offer a grunt or grumble. Or Piers would clear his throat and spit. But the three men shared no words amongst one another. For good reason. If the beast was near and heard them, they'd lose the only advantage they had, that the beast did not yet know they were coming.

The trees around them were old, taller than any he'd ever seen in all his years. They were like giants reaching high into the heavens. Standing beneath them even upon the back of his horse he felt as small and insignificant as an ant upon a man's arm. Their limbs were big and entwined with one another creating a dense canopy which blocked most of the sun's light from reaching the forest floor. Only occasionally would they walk through a small section of forest where the sun was shining through the leaves. But as quickly as the sun would touch him, it would retreat behind the dark curtain of leaves and the world would be cast in dark shadows once more.

A short while into their ride, they found the wyvern that Marcus had seen flying above them. The beast lay dead on the forest floor, the dark green scales of the beast ripped and torn by massive claws and its neck snapped nearly in two. The wyverns red eyes were lifeless orbs.

"Creator," Marcus heard Piers mutter as he glanced down at the still seeping claw woulds that had pierced the hard scales of the lesser dragon as if they had been little more than a stick of butter. "What kind of beast can kill a wyvern like that?"

"A very powerful one," Castron muttered. "Wyvern didn't even get the chance to fight back. No blood on the claws and no scorch marks of fire anywhere." The commander turned to him and said, "Be careful, Marcus. This just became much more dangerous." With his warning rattling in Marcus' brain, the old knight urged them to keep moving and continued on into the forest.

As he rode past the body of the wyvern, Marcus noticed a number of small roots and vines which seemed to be lying broken around the drake's body. He didn't know what it meant, or if the broken vines meant anything at all. But the knight still made note of it, truly believing it may be a clue to whatever was going on in this forest.

They walked through dense patches of underbrush, over small embankments, down gentle slopes and across small rippling streams. They encountered very few animals, save for crows and ravens, of which they saw plenty. It was eerily similar to the woods Marcus had noticed while they were riding to the town. Only these woods felt more oppressive, like an ancient spell or curse had been cast over it. This place didn't feel right.

Marcus found his eyes wandering this way and that, never truly able to remain upon the two knights as they rode before him. More than once he found himself heading in the opposite direction of the two men and had to quickly adjust course to rejoin them. They offered a few mocking glances at him each time it happened. But he didn't concern himself with those, mostly because there was something much more concerning that kept drawing his gaze.

A shadow was following them. A large being seemingly as tall as the very trees around him, enveloped in shadows, lurked in the darkest recesses of the forest. Wherever they moved the shadow seemed to as well. If they veered to the left, so did it. If they halted so Castron could decide where next to move, the shadow disappeared amongst the trees only to reappear as soon as their horses started moving once more. The way it walked almost seemed mocking to him, like it was moving so slowly because it knew he was watching but enjoyed toying with him. It almost felt like the shadow wanted him to see but did not want him to know what it was.

But that wasn't the part which concerned him. What concerned him was how the shadow was seemingly able to blend into the trees with ease. One moment he was looking at some sort of tall lumbering beast which walked with a shambling gait. The next, the shadow looked to be an abnormally large tree trunk rising high towards the heavens.

On more than one occasion he'd seen the shadow slowly following them on his right hand side, moving amidst the trees in that slow manner only for it to become lost amidst the trees. When he'd crane his head looking for it he'd soon find it walking on his left, shifting between the trees with an unnatural ease. Yet it still remained fair enough away that it was enveloped in shadows.

He should've said something to the knights, told them he'd seen the beast hidden in shadow. But he found himself unable to speak. Not out of fear of the beast, but out of fear that what he was seeing was all some trick of his mind. He wanted to be the one to find the beast and slay it. He wanted to prove that he deserved to be a Knight of the King. And in his desire to prove that, perhaps his mind perceived shadows of a lumbering beast where only tall trees hidden by shadow lurked. He had no way of knowing if what he saw was real or not. So he said nothing, hoping the beast would veer from the shadows enough so that he could see its true form.

Unfortunately, only once did he see the beast veer from its course as it followed them through the woods. Somewhere far off in the distance, the howl of a wolf split the silence hanging over the trees. At the sound the shadow had stopped abruptly and spun around, seemingly looking for the creature that had produced it.

The way it moved still did not reveal much about the beast as he'd hoped it would. But as the shadow turned and looked off in the opposite direction he saw something which made a lump form in his throat. Two large branching antlers like those of an elk extended from the side of what Marcus assumed was its head. They were massive, far larger than any antlers which could ever grow upon the head of any elk or moose.

The name of their god range out in his head like a warning bell. *Hernos the Horned One.* That's what Castron had told him the villagers of Dunwall believed their Old God was named. And whatever was following them, hidden by shadows, definitely seemed to be some sort of massive horned beast, just what he'd expect from a beast revered as a god.

As they seemed to get deeper and deeper into the wood, everything seemed to change. The limbs of the trees began to droop low. The ground beneath them seemed to grow more jagged and uneven with bulging tree roots which lay hidden beneath fallen leaves and creeping vines of ivy. The very air itself seemed to grow heavy. Though he wasn't sure if it just felt that way because of his own growing fears.

But when he turned to look for the shadow which had stalked them for so long and saw that it was gone, he knew something was wrong. They were getting close to something. He just wasn't sure what it was.

They had only walked for a few moments when Castron thrust his fist into the air and tugged the reins of his horse abruptly to stop it. The two of them managed to stop their horses before they could collide with one another. For the first time since they'd encountered the wyvern, Castron spoke. "I do not like this."

Marcus leaned in the saddle of his horse to look around the man and could not find the words to speak. Castron had made them read every book on creatures of Elesia at least twice. He'd stood before them and lectured them about the things that those creatures would do to a man when they killed them. He'd warned them about all the things they would see and smell when they saw their first victim of a monster.

But it still hadn't prepared him for what he saw.

There had been four villagers who had wandered out into the village that morning. Or Marcus assumed that there had been four. Because that's how many bodies they found. Three of them, all men, stood upon their feet, entangled within large pillars of what appeared to be abnormally large roots which had erupted from the earth at their feet, encased and trapped within them. With a single look Marcus could tell that it would be a great endeavor to cut the trees away from the bodies enough to free them from their imprisonment.

The bodies were mangled and broken, limbs snapped and broken and twisted in sickening ways that made him hope that they'd been dead before these horrors were committed upon them. The heads were even worse. They'd been partially caved in by the massive roots, spun and twisted and bent out of place, causing the bones of their necks to protrude from beneath the skin. It was a sight that made him want to vomit.

The fourth body, the body of a woman, at least appeared to have been spared the same gruesome death that had awaited the three men with her. The woman lay on her back near the feet of one of the men. From where he sat astride his horse, he couldn't help but think she looked like she was peacefully sleeping. But the sword wound in her chest told him otherwise.

He forced himself to look at the gruesome bodies of the men entangled within the tree branches, thinking that he must be missing something to explain why this one woman had died of a sword wound and the others hadn't. It didn't take long for him to notice the bloodied sword in the hand of the man whose feet she lay beside. Somehow he knew what had happened. He couldn't explain how he did. But Marcus was certain the man had driven his blade through the woman to spare her the agonizing death he and the other men had suffered. At least, that was the story that he was choosing to believe.

"This... this can't be possible," Piers mumbled weakly, his rough voice, typically so loud and booming, was soft and subdued in ways Marcus never knew it could be. It was almost as if the man was afraid. Marcus knew better than to ask him if he was. "I've never seen one before... I thought that they were myths. Or extinct."

"I had hoped beyond hope that we'd never see their kind again... but it appears my hope was not as strong as my faith," Castron offered with an unsatisfied shake of his head. He spun his horse around so that he could look directly at Marcus. "For all your thinking on the ride here have you any idea of a beast which can control the forests, summon great roots from the earth?" Marcus thought for a moment but quickly shook his head. "And what about beasts I didn't teach you much of? Beasts said only to live in myths and legends. Or beasts which we see so seldom that believe them to have gone extinct, become relics of the past which we must never forget. Know of any beasts which could do this?"

A chill gripped at his spine. He felt as if his stomach had already risen into his throat. There was only one such beast which was said to create pillars of trees and roots from the earth. Only one such beast which was said to be massively tall and could become lost within the trees. And it could do that because, unfortunately for them, the beast was born from trees.

Marcus struggled to speak the words. But somehow he managed to say them, though they lacked any conviction or strength. They were merely words which feel harmlessly from his mouth. But they were words which needed to be said. "A forest devil."

"Aye, that's what the people call them. But what do we call them?"

Even the word itself brought terror with it. But Marcus said it for the benefit of his commander. "Lesnik."

Castron nodded glumly. "We cannot stay in these woods for long. We must make haste back to the village. Swords will be worthless against this beast. So hurry. Back to Dunwall."

The commander spurred his horse and the two men followed after him. Marcus should have been relieved that they finally knew what manner of beast haunted these woods. But knowing it was a Lesnik brought no comfort or relief. They were said to be the trees given life, a protector of the forests which mercilessly killed any and all who dared threaten the forest. Legends said that the Lesnik could even control the trees themselves.

But the part that worried him most was that this was not a beast they could kill. He could chop the beast until it was nothing but dust and light the dust on fire. It would still return. Only then it would be more angry and vengeful.

The three men rode hard through the trees, trying to make it back to Dunwall before the beast could attack them. Of all the beasts he could've faced to prove he was worthy of being a Knight of the King, he ended up with one that couldn't be killed. Marcus sighed.

It figured.

CHAPTER 3

As soon as the trees fell away and the village of Dunwall was visible before them, all three men dared to breathe a sigh of relief. To survive in the forests with a Lesnik, even one that they had not provoked, was no easy feat.

So much so, in fact, that Marcus was fairly certain he'd heard Castron praying to the Creator for much of their frantic ride back through the forest. On more than one occasion Marcus had considered it himself but had quickly dismissed the idea. The Creator had done nothing for him but kill his mother and give him a father who wanted nothing to do with him. So what help would the God of Light truly be?

Castron led them across the small plain of tree stumps. The villagers who had gathered near the edge of the village were gone now, save for the woman who had begged them for help. She stood where they'd last seen her, blonde hair blowing in the gusty wind. Her baby was clutched tightly against her chest. As she stood, she bounced and moved gently about.

Marcus found himself staring at her as they rode back towards her. He wasn't sure if it was the emerald eyes hidden behind her blowing hair or the crooked smile that parted her lips as they approached. But the woman reminded him of his mother. A woman who had been gone for so very long he couldn't even remember the way that her hand had felt upon his skin, or even the sound of her voice. Most days it felt like she had only been a dream, a heavenly figure that walked in starlight. But worst of all, it was a dream that seemed to fade with time. But he could never forget the eyes of his mother, eyes that shined like emeralds, just as he'd never forget the way her crooked smile of pride made him feel. Somehow, this woman seemed to possess both.

She beckoned them and to Marcus's delight, Castron angled the horses towards her. As they slowly approached her, she called out to them softly. At first Marcus was confused by the softness of her voice. But when he allowed his eyes to take in everything before him, he realized that the woman's baby was sleeping in her arms. "Were you able to kill the beast?" she asked.

His heart sank. There was such optimism in her voice, so much hope that the very idea of telling this woman they could not kill the creature haunting these woods like a plague was not pleasant. He wanted to help her anyway he could. Not only because she reminded him of his mother, but because of the babe clutched in her arms. The child did not deserve to live her life in constant fear of a demon in the forests. They needed to deal with it. Whatever the cost.

Castron's face was solemn. Marcus suspected that the old man, as heartless as the knights who trained under him claimed him to be, was feeling the same sorrow that he was. "I'm afraid it is not that simple, m'lady. I wish I could say more but we must speak to the chieftain at once. Has he returned yet?"

She nodded and somehow the look of fear and despair upon her face made Marcus' heart feel even heavier. Somehow she could see right through Castron's avoidance. She could tell that things were far direr than any of them had realized just by their answer. But she did not question them on it. Either because she did not think the men wanted to tell her. Or because she was afraid to know the truth.

"Where can we find him?" Castron asked.

"Follow me," she said as she turned sharply on her heels and began to make her way back towards the village.

Castron slid gracefully from the saddle of his horse and Marcus did as he did. As soon as his feet hit the soft grass, he was shocked at how foreign standing felt to his feet. He'd been riding the horse for so long that his legs could hardly remember what it felt like to stand. He stretched, trying to loosen his stuff muscles and aching bones. But Castron and Piers were already following after the woman. He grumbled under his breath, grabbed hold of the reins and followed after them as quickly as his weary legs would carry him.

As they walked along the trampled grass trails, Marcus could hardly believe what he was seeing. Because he saw nothing. Every house was sealed shut. The doors closed, shutters pulled closed over the windows. Not a single person was outside of their home, save for the four of them as they made their way towards the chieftain's home.

"Where are all the villagers?" Marcus called from the rear of the group, intrigue getting the better of him. "Have they already retreated to their homes for the night?"

Marcus heard her chuckle even from where he was, as if she was amused by the question itself. But once she spoke he realized that wasn't exactly the case. "I didn't know you could speak other than to tell the old women you hoped our beast would kill her."

"I speak well enough. Though I do find it easier to threaten old women with death than I do to speak to pretty women like yourself."

"You flatter me knight."

"I'm not a knight," he admitted somewhat shamefully. "This is my test to become one. If I can stop this creature, then you can call me a knight."

"Then let us hope that you stop this creature, for both our sakes," she called from the front of the group without looking back at him. She led them between two houses and then her voice rang out once more. "The chieftain lives there."

The chieftain's house was, for the most part, the same as the other homes of the village except with a few major exceptions. A rudimentary home made from wood with a thatched roof stood before them with the shutters drawn over the windows. Had that been all they saw, Marcus wouldn't have been angry. A chieftain living as the other villagers did would have been a sign of unity telling his villagers that he was one of them. He suffered the same as they did.

But when Marcus saw that the home had been expanded in three different ways, almost as if they had built three more separate houses on the sides and then combined all of them into one gigantic home, he grew angry. And he grew even angrier when he began to realize that the trees the villagers had been clearing had been used to construct the extravagant additions to the chieftain's home. The more he thought about it, the more he found his hands trembling with unbridled rage.

He'd brought the beast down upon them. It was his doing.

His thoughts were scrambled when he heard Castron's voice again. "Thank you, m'lady. But I have one more request to ask of you."

"You may request it," she said formally, though Marcus was wise enough to know that the 'request' Castron spoke of was not one she could refuse. And based upon the stiffness of her response, he suspected that she knew it too.

"Marcus needs to speak to someone who knows much about the village, ask some questions about the villagers," the commander said. "You seem a fine choice for such a thing. Would you speak to Marcus, answer his questions?"

The woman looked to him as he sat astride his horse, gently patting her on the side of the neck. "He may follow me to my home if he wishes. We can speak there."

Before Marcus had the chance to tell Castron that he believed Piers would have been better at the task, the old commander spun about in the saddle quickly and gave him orders that Marcus was convinced would have been better served by Piers. "Follow her back to her home. Ask her about the mark. See if she's seen anyone who might have it."

Marcus gave the old man a respectful bow. "As you command."

He slipped out of the saddle as they drew nearer to the chieftain's home. The knights led their horses towards the chieftain's home and tied their horse off to a different wooden column which had been erected to support a slanted roof. As the old man and Piers made their way up the wooden stairs to the chieftain's porch, Marcus made his way back to the woman as she smiled at him.

She did not delay a moment and began to make her way through the village. All of the houses were dark, their candles and torches either snuffed out or concealed by the shutters that covered the windows. As they walked, the woman picked twigs and branches out of the tangled mess of shaggy black hair upon his head. She tried to make small talk as they walked, asking about his training and things of little consequence. Marcus tried to answer her questions as best as he could. But with his thoughts plagued by the shadowy thing that had stalked them through the woods and learning that the beast was a Lesnik, he was sure he wasn't good company.

The sky was darkening, the sun creeping ever lower in the sky. There was a chill on the air. But that was to be expected these days. Winter had arrived and with it, cold snowy nights would soon follow. He hated the winters in the barracks at their fortress. The wooden slat walls did little to keep the cold out. He'd always longed to sleep in the stone fortress, always believing it had to be warmer than the wooden barracks. But just a few nights prior, they'd allowed him to sleep in the fortress to get a good night's rest before they embarked on this journey to kill the beast. To his surprise, the fortress had been nearly as cold as the barracks.

She led him back towards the heart of the village, weaving between buildings seemingly at random. After a while, she seemed to stop talking. He noticed that she seemed to be looking back over her shoulders in paranoia but decided it was best to not ask her about it. He followed her in silence as she crept her way between the houses.

Her house was on the edge of the village, the door facing out into the forest. He followed her inside her home and watched as she crossed the main room and lay the baby down in a small wooden cradle near the fireplace. The flames within the stone hearth cast the entire room in orange light. As the woman walked about in the home, searching for something amidst the shelves on the wall furthest from him, he allowed himself to look around the sparsely furnished home. He saw a small table with two chairs around it and noticed that one of the chairs was coated in a heavy layer of dust from lack of use. On a bookshelf near the table, an old axe, the blade weathered and nicked from age and hard use.

Marcus knew he shouldn't have. But he crossed the room and made his way over to the bookshelf. He grabbed the axe from the shelf and held it tightly in his hands. The wooden handle was still sturdy and the blade, for all its faults, was still sharp enough that when he ran his finger along it, it split the skin open with ease. A woodcutter's axe.

"It is... It was my husband's axe," he heard the woman call out. He turned to look at her, the axe still held firmly in his hands, as she approached with two clay cups in her hands. "He used to cut wood for the town so we could stay warm in the winter. He... was one of the first that the creature in the woods killed."

"I'm sorry," was all the man could manage to say. He gently placed the axe back on the shelf where she'd left it, hoping he hadn't offended her by holding it.

"What's happened was meant to happen," she said somberly as she placed the two cups down on the small table and sat down in the chair which was not covered in dust, "which is an expression of faith in the divine power and workings of the Creator and the nature of this world." She beckoned for him to take a seat in the dust covered chair. "My husband was meant to die so that you and the other knights would come here so that others did not have to."

Marcus took a seat in the dust covered chair. "Do you truly believe that? That the Creator wanted your husband to die so that we could help you?"

"What I believe... I want to believe that to be truth... I want to believe that the Creator took my husband to the Halls of his Father so that others did not need to suffer. Whether it is true or not, I'll never know. But it is what I choose to believe... because if I don't... and my husband died for nothing, for no reason..."

He bit his tongue. He'd always believed that the truth was more important than faith. But telling the woman the truth, that her husband had been killed because he cut down trees and had been one of the main reasons the Lesnik had even begun attacking, would only bring her more sorrow. And what good was the truth if it broke someone's heart?

"We know what the beast is that killed your husband and we know how to stop it. But I need your help to do it," he said, allowing the truth to remain hidden.

The sorrow disappeared from her face as soon as he began to speak. The emerald green eyes seemed to glow with happiness. She looked a different woman and Marcus couldn't help but take notice. "Whatever help you need, ask it. I'll do whatever you need."

"Have you ever heard of a Lesnik?" She shook her head. "Do you know what the legends say about what happens when men start clearing the forests?"

"The forest fights back," she answered. "My husband used to speak of that often. Tell stories that his father and grandfather had told him about man getting too greedy, cutting the trees down to expand villages and provoking the wrath of the trees. It was why he only cut down what was needed to keep the village warm. He feared the wrath of the forest."

"Unfortunately your chieftain didn't," Marcus said without even trying to hide the disgust he felt towards the man. "His clearing of the trees caused a Lesnik, a forest demon, to awaken. It's an ancient beast, the trees given life and form. It's what haunts your woods. They're nearly impossible to kill and they live only to kill all who would bring harm upon the trees."

"It's impossible to kill?" she asked. Marcus nodded glumly. "Then how do you plan to stop it?"

"Legends claim that it does something which we call 'marking'," he explained slowly, trying to find the right words to say to the woman. If he explained too much, he couldn't be sure she'd agree to help him if she knew that he would need to kill someone in the village to stop the Lesnik, even if it meant saving it. So he mulled the words carefully before he spoke. "It places a strange rash upon the skin of someone who lives in the area near the forest which it is protecting. A bark skin rash the legends call it. They say it looks like tree bark has grown into the skin."

Marcus watched the woman as her eyes grew wide. Her eyes looked everywhere but towards him. Often times they strayed in the direction of her bed. A sheen of sweat formed on her forehead which she tried desperately to wipe away with her hand. But it seemed to return as quickly as she wiped it away. Even her posture, once so relaxed and subdued as she'd sat at the table across from him calmly drinking from her clay cup had shifted. She looked a feral cat ready to pounce, arms tense and rigid, fists clenched so tightly all the color seemed to have drained from her hands.

Silence grew in the room, only broken by the occasional crackle of the fire burning in the hearth. And it lingered long as the two of them sat, one trembling slightly as she looked around wildly, frantically, while the other sat calmly, watching her, trying in vain to understand what was happening or why she'd suddenly begun acting so strange.

Once the silence grew uncomfortable, he waited a few moments longer. Finally, he decided he could not stand it any longer. "The bark skin rash, it's the only way we can stop the Lesnik. We just..."

"I don't care about the rash," she snapped back fiercely. The manner with which she had said it, erupting with unwarranted anger like a volcano of fire and destruction, told Marcus everything that the silence had not.

"You know the one who has the bark skin rash, don't you?" he asked, though it was less of a question and more of a statement. Whether she answered or not, it did not matter. He thought about pressing her for answers, moving the chair closer to her and asking her questions until she grew tired of listening to them. She knew the person that the Lesnik had marked. She could help him stop the creature as she claimed she wanted to.

But he was never given the chance to question her.

The door to her home thundered loudly under an onslaught of knocking fists. Whoever stood on the other side of the door was striking the wood with such force and authority he couldn't actually believe they hadn't knocked the door free from the rusted hinges that held it. The woman sat stone like in her chair, frightened. So Marcus rose and went to the door.

When he opened it, he found himself looking at the gruff faces of Castron and Piers. Behind them stood a man he recognized as an apothecary, given the dark robes which covered his whole body and the long, beak nosed mask which graced his face. The beak nosed man carried a large leather book in his hands. Marcus knew the book but not why the man held it. The two knights looked frazzled, their faces some strange mixture of sympathy and relief.

The commander ran his hand through his white hair nervously and let out a deep sign. He taped the handle of his sword anxiously. "We need to talk."

CHAPTER 4

astron pushed passed him before he even had time to utter a reply, Piers and the apothecary filing into the house on his heels. There was something about the three men that didn't sit well with Marcus. They seemed to be in a frenzy, rushing around quickly without communicating what was happening. Castron had always told them that communication between fellow knights was the most important part of any given hunt for a beast. Communication ensured that everyone knew the plan and would stick to it when swords were drawn and blood was shed. But it seemed that his commander and sword master had forgotten that lesson.

The three men crossed the room and headed directly towards the woman as she sat at the table. Her eyes were darting between those approaching her and the woodcutter's axe which sat upon a shelf a few paces from where she sat.

Marcus could already see the situation escalating, especially if the woman made even the slightest indication that she was going to make a move towards her husband's axe. Castron and Piers would not take such an act kindly. If she even took a step towards the axe, blades would be drawn and an already hostile situation would turn violent before long.

So Marcus scurried past the approaching men as quickly as he could and placed himself directly between the approaching group and the worried woman whose eyes seemed to be lingering longer on the axe than they did on the group.

"Out of the way boy," Castron ordered sternly.

Marcus, however, disobeyed the man's orders and remained where he was. It was foolish to disobey the commander's decree and even more foolish to do so when he had yet to be made a knight. But in that moment he didn't care. He wanted to avoid making an already bad situation even worse. So he remained where he was, between them, rooted to the spot like one of the hundreds of trees that surrounded the village. "Not until you tell me what's going on."

The commander held out his calloused hand and the apothecary seemed to understand what the gesture meant. He walked forward and placed the old leather book in Castron's waiting hand. The old man raised the book towards Marcus, as if the worn and partially destroyed leather book was the best answer he could give. "You know this book, do you not?"

"Don't insult me," Marcus fired back without thinking. He needed to watch his tone with the commander. "That's the bestiary of the Knights of the King. It's the tome you made us read from time and again. It's the tome which taught us all we know of the beasts in these lands, compiled through the ages by the wisest knights. Why do you need it?"

"There is a passage about Lesniks within…"

"I know about Lesniks. I've read the passages same as you commander."

"It's not for you." The old man's gruff voice caught him off guard. "It's for her. She's the marked one. She's the bark skin rash."

He glanced back at her over his shoulder, trying to study her somber face. But for all his efforts, he couldn't decide if the commander spoke true, or if something else was happening here that he did not yet understand. Perhaps this was a further test that the elder knights were thrusting upon him. He didn't know.

But he was certain that the woman was not the one who bore the bark skin mark upon her flesh.

But... was he certain of that? Did he truly know that the woman before him did not have the rash upon her? Or did he just want so badly for her to not have the rash that he was convincing himself that she didn't? She had acted strangely when he'd mentioned it...

He did not know. So he offered the only protest he could. "You lie." But for all the accusations he wished to throw at the commander, for all the doubt and anger and defiance he felt towards them for barging into the woman's home and accusing her of such a terrible thing, his words were not strong. They fell weakly from his mouth, no strength or force of will behind them. They were meaningless words that gave away his waning convictions.

"The only lies being spoken in this room are the ones you tell yourself boy," the old knight said sharply. "The bark skin rash tends to manifest itself upon the arm. You know this. Have you seen her arms? Have you yet seen her without her dress on?"

Marcus knew not how to respond. He hadn't seen her without her brown dress on. Though he'd have been lying if he said he hadn't wished she'd take it off. The skirt covered her legs and the long sleeves hid her arms from view. But winter was setting in. Winter brought with it cold and the day had been chilly which meant the night would be cold. How could he take her clothing to mean she was guilty of possessing the mark they claimed she did? This wasn't the king's justice. This was something else. There was no justice to be found in this home now, only accusations and finger pointing without proof. And he was not going to allow it to continue.

"Are we to condemn the whole village then, unless they agree to walk naked before us to prove that they don't have the bark skin mark?" he asked sharply, no longer attempting to hide the barely restrained fury in his voice. "Perhaps you'd just like to kill the whole village while we're at it commander. Can't take any chances now can we? Kill them all and burn it to the ground.

We'll make the beast go away before it can claim the corpses of this place."

Castron's face glowed red with fury to match Marcus's. But the old knight, the wise man that he was, did not allow himself to speak in anger. Instead, he turned to look at the apothecary. With a grunt and a nod, he bequeathed the apothecary the right to speak. It was a right that the beak nosed man did not seem keen to let pass. He took a few steps towards Marcus but was quickly pulled back by Piers. The sword master must have seen the violent explosion brewing within him. Had he allowed the apothecary to reach him, Marcus surely would've beat the man senseless. Not necessarily because of the man himself. It was more because he could not strike either of the knights without risking his life.

"She's a strange rash upon her skin," the beak nosed man said, his voice distorted and hollow sounding as it bounced and rattled in the hollowed out space that was the beak. "Some days back, must've been the day that the forest started killing folk, Kyia approached me and asked for salves and poultices to put upon a strange rash she'd noticed just that morning. I asked to see it but she refused. No others have come to me about a rash. Only her."

"Circumstantial at best," Marcus said dismissively. "If a snake bites a horse in the leg and the rider dies you think you can blame the snake?" he continued, trying to remember the words about Lesniks which he'd read in the weathered book of leather which Castron still clutched tightly. "The same goes here. Just because she has a rash does not mean it is the bark skin." Damn it. Why couldn't he remember what the book said?

The old knight grumbled. "You defend her so, Marcus. Yet you do not turn and ask her if she possesses the bark skin rash. Why is that? Why do you not ask her? Because you're afraid that she may have the rash? Or because you already know that she does and refuse to believe it?"

Marcus fell silent. For once he did not know the right thing to say to the old knight. He could've asked her at any moment if she had the bark skin. Yet he hadn't. Why hadn't he? Was it because he didn't want to know the truth? Or was it because he already knew the truth? Even if the old man was right, even if she did possess the bark skin upon her, he was not going to let them kill her. The woman had a baby. He'd find another way. Even if it killed him, he'd find a way to spare this woman her life.

"I'm sorry commander... But it matters not to me if she has the rash or not... I'm not going to let you kill her," Marcus said defiantly, puffing his chest out in a mock showing of strength and force. "We will find another way if we have to. But you'll not kill her like this." There was another way in the bestiary. He knew it. But he couldn't remember it.

The look of disappointment upon the old knight's face cut through him like a rusty dagger, leaving a gaping wound which seemed to fester with more pain the longer it remained. And Castron's look seemed to linger long, carving him time and time again until it felt as if his body had become one festering wound of disappointment which would never heal. He'd failed the commander. He'd let the man down. A smart man would've stepped aside and tried to make the old man beam with pride as he'd done earlier that very day.

But Marcus would do no such thing. He remained there like the tree he'd become. He did not waver and he did not move. He blocked the girl from the men and he'd not stop.

"Piers," the sullen and disappointed voice of the gruff old man rang out in the small room, "restrain Marcus while we tend to the marked one."

In the time it took him to hear and process what the commander's orders had meant, it was too late. He felt Pier's strong and battle scarred hands clench tightly around his upper arms, felt his arms being pulled back behind him, away from his steel and, even worse, away from the commander and the apothecary as they sauntered passed him towards the girl called Kyia.

The girl tried to retreat but there was nowhere to go. The back wall of her home and the bookshelf where the axe lay loomed large behind her. She turned to look at the axe once but then her eyes drifted to Marcus, almost for reassurance that she was doing the right thing. Luckily, when he gave her a wide eyed shake of the head, she seemed to abandon the idea and tried to slip between the two men as they closed in on her.

The commander did not make a move to grab her as she tried to race through the narrow gap between him and the apothecary. Marcus expected as much. He'd once watched Castron beat a knight nearly to death for trying to force a young woman to let him take her to his bed. When she'd refused, he'd grabbed her arm so tightly that, after a week of healing, she joked that a palm reader could've told the man's fortune by looking at her arm. Castron had seen the offense and erupted with raw anger. After he'd exiled the bloodied and bruised knight to the Exiled Lands north of their kingdom, he'd made it clear that no man was to lay hands upon a man or woman unless they posed a threat to their life. He claimed that they were knights, not barbarians or common bandits. They were to be better. And they would be better. Or else.

But the apothecary was not a knight, nor was he bound by the rules which Castron had so angrily established that haunting day. He lunged for the woman. By some stroke of dumb luck, he managed to entangle his fingers in the billowing cloth of her dress. He struggled against her as she tried to pull free of his grasp. But he slowly balled more and more of the dress up in his hand until he managed to pull her close enough to grab hold of her.

She didn't seem to struggle as the apothecary wrapped his arms around her, effectively trapping her in his grasp. She seemed resigned to her fate.

Marcus, however, was not going to let this happen without putting on a struggle. He pulled and thrashed and jerked. He pleaded with Piers. He begged the man to let him go, to stop what was happening because they both knew it wasn't right. But Piers refused to disobey his commander. On one occasion Marcus nearly broke free of the sword master's grasp. But in his surprise at breaking free, he stumbled enough to let the man reaffirm his grip and Marcus was restrained once more.

He could only watch as the commander approached the lady. The old man asked the woman if he could look at her arms. Marcus wasn't sure if she'd given him a response. It wouldn't have mattered anyways. The commander was going to check for the bark skin mark with or without her permission. As anger and anguish seemed to drape over him like a shroud, he began to thrash around even harder as Castron rolled up the sleeves of her dress and carefully looked over her arms.

It was agonizing being forced to stand by and watch as the commander looked the woman over carefully. Only a moment or two had passed but it felt like days were passing by slowly as the old man turned her arms every which way that he could. The longer he looked, the more confused his commander seemed to grow. And the angrier Marcus grew. The commander was searching harder than he should've had to. He wanted her to be the marked one. It was the only reason that made any sense.

But all the anger seemed to disappear when Castron rolled the woman's sleeves down and said, "I am sorry that I doubted you, m'lady. You do not have the mark. Forgive me for our intrusion. But the apothecary seemed certain it was you."

The apothecary offered a protest to the commander's words, seemingly bothered by the fact that it was his wrongdoing which had created such a tense and hostile situation. The two men began to bicker and argue about something that Marcus wasn't really listening to. In that moment, all he could do was look at the woman and smile. He'd believed in her and he'd been right to. She wasn't hiding the marking they were looking for.

However, the arguing in the room did not last for long. A sound cut through the air and silenced the whole room. As soon as Marcus heard it the air was ripped from his lungs. Fear gripped at his heart. It was a sound that, in all the commotion and tense moments they'd just gotten through, he had not expected to hear. And it was the last sound he'd hoped to hear.

Marcus turned to look at Kyia still clutched tightly in the apothecary's grasp. For the first time since he'd met her, he saw true panic in her eyes. In that moment he knew. He understood everything that had happened. And in a few moments, everyone else would too.

They would know that the crying baby had the bark skin rash upon her flesh.

Castron turned to look at the small crib Marcus had seen the woman put the baby to sleep in. He hesitated a moment, almost afraid to approach it in fear of what he might find. But the old man steadied himself. With a heavy reluctant sigh he strode across the room slowly, approaching the crib with such trepidation, Marcus wondered if the man thought a beast might lunge from within the crib and attack him.

Kyia tried to break free of the apothecary's grasp. She wasn't strong enough to do so. She pleaded with Castron to not approach the babe. The man turned her down time and time again, offering weak condolences and repeatedly saying he was only doing his duty. With each failed attempt at getting to the baby, she grew more frenzied. Tears streamed down her cheeks, flying off her face as she flailed emotionally about.

Marcus could not even find the strength to move. Piers' grip remained on his arms but the man could've been ten strides away and he still wouldn't have been able to move. Everything seemed to be spiraling out of control so fast he could barely keep his thoughts straight. One moment he was in fear that they were going to kill the woman. Next, euphoria that she wasn't the marked one. Then... this.

He watched, numb to nearly everything, as Castron stood before the small crib. He looked down into the crib and his hard face, the stoic and unflinching strength he always seemed to wear upon his brow, broke. Marcus could've sworn he saw a tear sting at the corner of the man's eye as he lifted the crying girl from the crib and pulled one of her arms away from her chest with gentle hands.

There, upon her flesh was the mark, a patch of skin which looked to have become dark and rough like the bark of a tree. The mark of the Lesnik.

Castron's face was distraught as he lay the small child back into the crib. But it was nowhere near as pained and agonizing as the look which graced Kyia's face. She wailed and sobbed, pleading, begging. She offered the man anything. She offered to leave the town, to take the babe far away from Dunwall if that would mean the Lesnik would be appeased. But Castron said nothing in reply. He stared down at the crib, seemingly undecided what he would do.

A voice called out then, the last voice Marcus wanted to hear. "You know what must be done, knight commander," the apothecary's hollow voice seemed to reverberate within his mask. "You said so yourself. The only way to save the village is to kill the one who bears the mark. If it is not done, it'll kill until the whole village is dead. Is the life of one babe worth more than the lives of the dozens of families who live here?"

"Castron," Marcus pleaded as soon as the man stopped talking. If he did not say anything and allowed the apothecary's words be the last he heard before he made his decision, Castron may have felt compelled to do as the apothecary wanted. But Marcus was not going to allow the commander to kill the babe with a clear conscious and the belief that he was doing the right thing. "Commander, you told us that knights do not to harm the innocent. That baby is innocent. She'd done nothing wrong. We can find a way to help her. But if you kill her, you're killing an innocent baby who never did anything wrong. What would your Creator think of such an act? Do you honestly think he would condone that?" Castron did not flinch, his vacant eyes staring down into the crib. "Damn it commander, look at me! Look at Kyia! This is wrong."

"There is no other way, Marcus. None that we know to actually work without drawing the wrath of the beast down on the village... This is the only way." The old man's voice had never been so small and hollow. "The Creator knows this is the way of the world. He knows that sometimes men must do terrible things to the few in order to protect the many. So while he may not condone this... he will understand. At least... I hope he will understand."

The old man hesitated for a long while, seemingly in quiet contemplation, trying to convince himself that there was some truth to the words he had said. As Kyia continued her frantic pleading through free-flowing tears of sorrow, Castron drew a small dagger with a long, thin blade which came to a wicked sharp point from his belt.

Marcus searched within himself for the strength to do what he knew he needed to do. If he did what his heart was telling him to do, he would never become a Knight of the King. If he acted upon the urges growing within him, he would probably be put to death at the edge of Castron's blade before the night was through. So he needed to be sure that this was what he wanted to do. He needed to be sure he was ready to throw his life away for Kyia and the baby.

There was no hesitation in him that day. There was right and there was wrong. What Castron was preparing to do was wrong. And he was not going to allow it to happen.

Marcus threw his head backwards as hard as he could, so hard that he felt like his neck might snap as he did it. He felt the back of his head slam against Piers' face, heard a strange snapping sound which he took to mean he'd broken the sword master's nose, then felt the man's hands grow lax on his arm as his body crumbled to the floor.

He would not hesitate. He broke into a sprint towards the commander as he stood next to the small crib, knife still in hand, hesitating to do what he thought he needed to do.

Castron turned his head just in time to see Marcus throw all his weight into the man's side. The old man let out a sharp grunt in pain and the two men went tumbling to the floor. The dagger slipped from Castron's grasp and skittered off into a dark corner of the room.

Marcus pushed himself quickly to his feet and raced towards the apothecary. The man tried to push Kyia away to protect himself but he had waited a moment too long. Marcus' fist collided with the beak-nosed mask upon his face and the wood splintered in two. The apothecary was spun by the blow and by the time he'd righted himself, Marcus had drawn his sword. With his hands clenched tightly around the blade, he swung. The pommel struck the apothecary across the cheek and the man fell immediately, not to stir again for some time.

Out of the corner of his eye he saw Castron crawling across the floor towards the knife, which was just barely out of his reach now. Marcus was not going to give him the chance to get it. He tossed his sword aside and leapt, landing hard on the wooden floor beside the commander as his hand wrapped around the handle of the knife. Marcus clasped both hands around the blade and the two men began to grapple for control of the dagger. Each tug, be it his own of the commander's, seemed to force the blade to cut deeper and deeper into the flesh of his palms.

But he wasn't going to let go.

The commander forced himself to his feet and Marcus did the same, both men refusing to let go of the dagger. The commander kicked at him but Marcus avoided the blow. "This is madness boy... I don't know what you think you're doing. But if you interfere with what needs to be done again, you'll be lucky if you've a head by the time the sun sets," Castron snarled through labored breaths of exertion, his face contorted into that angry look that made men pray.

But Marcus did not pray. Instead, he removed one of his hands from the blade and threw blood towards the commander's face. The man recoiled, his grip on the dagger loosening. As he tumbled backwards Marcus ripped the blade from his commander's hand and tossed it out the open window into the grassy walkways outside.

"Kyia, take the baby! Hide!" he yelled, struggling to keep his feet from the exertion of the melee with the commander. His hands throbbed with intense pain, blood seeping freely from the sword wounds to his palms. He gasped, trying to catch his breath.

He saw Kyia racing towards the door, the small child clutched tightly against her chest as he stumbled over to his fallen sword and slid it back into the scabbard at his waist. Piers was still lying in a daze on the floor, his nose bleeding, though it looked to him that the sword master was well enough to fight and had simply chosen not to. But Castron, the old fool that he was, had already risen to his feet and was staggering towards the door to follow after Kyia, a hand pressed against the side where Marcus had sent him sprawling.

Marcus knew it was the most reckless thing he would ever do. But he charged the commander once more. He threw all his weight into the man's turned back and the two of them were sprawling again, tumbling out the open door and into the slowly darkening night sky. Marcus tried to rise to his feet quickly but the dewy grass made his feet slip and he was on his back again.

He pushed himself to his knees and saw the commander was already on his feet, sword drawn and held on high. "Draw your sword." The words were an order, a command that he was to follow. But Marcus offered him no such satisfaction. He laughed at the old man and rose to his feet slowly, sword still snuggly in its scabbard. "I said draw your sword," he hissed again.

"I'm not going to fight you commander," Marcus said with as much feigned respect as he could muster in his anger. "There's another way to help her without killing a baby. And if you think that fighting me will make it so that you're right on this, then I'll not draw steel. Because you're wrong commander. And you know it."

"It is unwise to disobey my orders on your first quest to become a Knight of the King. I do not take kindly to men who disobey orders. Now, draw your sword." The commander trembled with anger as he held the blade, his face flush and beat red.

"Is that an order?" Marcus asked.

"Yes."

"Guess I'm disobeying that one too then."

"So be it." Castron surged forward and struck, his blade rending air as it circled towards Marcus in a looping arc that would have cut his head off if he hadn't ducked with the unnatural quickness he'd been gifted at birth. The old man quickly reversed his strike, hurtling the blade towards Marcus once more. He scampered to the side and the blade struck the grass where he had once stood.

Castron swung again, catching Marcus flat footed. He couldn't move away from the cut quick enough. So he did the only thing he could think to do. He drew his blade and deflected the attack. Castron's sword seemed to whine when their blades met on edge. As Marcus pushed away, the old man stumbled again, his feet slipping on the dewy grass as he toppled over.

Marcus made a move to help the man to his feet but he hesitated. The man was madder than he'd ever seen him before. He knew the old man would not see fit to accept his offering to help. So he remained where he was, watching as the grumbling old man managed to rise to a knee and glare at him with murderous intent.

"Do you know that they say I'm the godliest man you'll ever meet?" the commander asked with short raspy breaths. He pushed himself to his feet, struggling under the exertion. Marcus gave no answer. "Because when men see my sword, they pray. They pray to every god that there ever was and ever will be. They pray that I will see fit to give them a quick death."

"You aren't going to kill me." The words came out more confident than Marcus actually felt. But he'd not give the commander the satisfaction. As vicious and frenzied as Castron's attacks had been, the man was pulling his punches, so to speak. Each blow would have struck his gambeson or chainmail. They would've hurt like hell, maybe even knocked the wind right from his lungs. But they wouldn't have killed him. "So don't expect any prayers."

"You're an insolent little shit who does not yet know his place," Castron said sharply. "I am commander of the Knights of the King and you are..."

"The only one doing the right thing. It wouldn't matter if you were commander of the Knights of the King or the King of Elesia, you'd still be wrong. Any man willing to sacrifice a baby without even trying to find another way... that's not a man I can follow. If that is truly who you are, if this is what you will ask me to do someday... Then I don't want this. I don't want to be like you."

Castron's face fell for a moment. Disappointment etched upon his brow. But it lingered for only the briefest of moments. And then the anger returned. "If you do not have the courage to do what must be done then perhaps you should never have been a knight to begin with."

The words cut through him more swiftly and viciously than any he'd ever felt before, carving him to pieces as he stood and looked at the old man he'd once respected. He'd been forced to join their ranks ten years before. He'd been forced to train and learn under these men for all those years. And now, when he was on the cusp of becoming a knight, the commander was telling him he did not have what it took to be a knight. Because he desired to do what he felt was right.

"You'd kill a baby when this is no fault of hers?" Marcus asked. "This mess is the doing of the chieftain, not her. If you're going to kill someone, he's the one that should die for this. He's the one who had the trees cut down. He caused all this. He's the monster that caused this beast to mark her. She's innocent. We need to save her."

"Doesn't matter," Castron replied, bristling with anger. "She's the one that's been marked. We can't save her. Killing the chieftain will achieve nothing. Killing the girl will save countless lives."

"If you think I'll let you do anything to that baby, you're wrong," Marcus said defiantly. "Anything that happens to her will have to happen to me first."

"She won't feel a thing. I can't say the same for you," Castron snarled in anger.

Marcus knew that Castron meant the words as some form of comfort, hoping that he would understand the baby wouldn't suffer while he was 'saving the town' as the commander claimed he was. But he could not take them that way.

Something snapped within him. An unrestrained fury that had been brewing just below the surface seemed to be unleashed at the words. He saw red, felt a surge of energy and adrenaline fill his arms. Anger and hatred that hadn't been on his mind a moment before seemed to consume his thoughts as he charged at his commander in a blind rage.

The old man raised his sword and held it defensively as Marcus's blade slashed wildly through the air, flailing about without any semblance of form. His blade keened and whined and clanged as it bashed violently against the old man's as he tried desperately to block each of the blows that Marcus sent his way. Somehow, he did. But the man was losing ground and strength with each blow he blocked. With each clash, his arms seemed to tremble a little more, his grip seemed to weaken. His body was breaking faster than his calm resolve and steely will.

A powerful overhead strike sent the commander down to one knee, struggling to keep his blade held high to defend himself.

Marcus sent a looping cut towards the man's blade, and in that moment, the old man's body broke. His grip weakened. As soon as the two blades collided, the sword was thrown from the commander's hand and he was knocked to his back. It fell weakly to the grass outside of Castron's reach as the old man looked up at him with wild and bewildered eyes.

Marcus did not say a word as he looked down at the old man. He sheathed his sword and turned his back to leave the commander lying in the grass when he heard the old man call out weakly, "There's a demon within you boy. A monster waiting for an excuse to be unleashed on this world."

Marcus did not humor him with a reply. He continued walking away from the scene of the brutal fight he'd gotten in with the man who would no longer be his commander. After what he'd just done, there was no going back. He'd never be a Knight of the King. Not anymore.

"Your father was a good man and your grandfather, even more so. So the words I say to you now, I say because of the men who came before you. You've until the moon is high in the sky to get your head on right. What has happened here... it is not too late to be forgiven. But you need to get your head on straight if you truly wish to be a knight, boy."

At that, Marcus stopped and turned to face the old man. "If

you had been the one to disarm me and I had lost our fight, would you still have offered me such a deal? Would you have claimed these actions could be forgiven?" The old man's silence was all the answer that Marcus needed. "That's what I thought."

Marcus resumed walking away from Castron, though it felt like he was walking away from a lot more than that. It felt like he was turning his back on his chance to be a Knight of the King. He was turning his back on the only future he could ever remember wanting. It was all because he could not find the strength to kill a baby to save the rest of these villagers from the Lesnik. All he had to do was let the commander kill the child and he could be a Knight of the King, prevent such tragedies from ever happening again. By turning a blind eye and pretending that he was doing the right thing, he could be a knight. And then hope that maybe someday, he'd believe he had actually done the right thing.

But Marcus kept walking. He would never be a Knight of the King. He knew that and he did not care. In that moment, only a single thought drove him. He needed to find Kyia and the baby before anyone else did.

He was going to protect them. He would make sure that the two of them lived to see another day. He swore the oath to whatever being was willing to listen. He would protect them or he would die trying. This was his oath.

And he would keep it.

CHAPTER 5

He scoured the village for some time, looking behind every corner of every house, inside every wooden barrel he spotted and even behind every pile of chopped firewood stacked at the backs of the small huts. He'd nearly given up hope when she'd crawled out from behind a large stack of hay bales and dragged him into the small gap between the hay and a home where she'd taken to hiding.

"You didn't have to do that," she whispered. "You struck your commander for..."

"He's not my commander," he said sharply, cutting her off before she could finish. He knew it wasn't right to be so short with her. It had been his choice which had cost him the chance to become a knight, not hers. He tried to calm himself as he spoke, though he wasn't sure the ocean could quench the raging fire the commander's actions had sparked within him. "He never will be my commander after what I did. So let's not speak of it any more."

She nodded weakly in understanding as she bounced the baby in her arms, intent to keep her from waking and giving away her hiding spot. "What do you intend to do?"

Marcus already had something of a plan. It wasn't a great plan nor was it particularly smart. But it was the best plan that he'd been able to come up with as he roamed the village searching for her, trying to keep himself hidden by the shadows as much as he could so as to not raise any unneeded suspicions. He especially needed to avoid the eyes of the knights and the apothecary, three men who would surely follow him back to the woman. He couldn't allow that.

"Is there a home where you can hide?" he asked. "A friend who can keep you hidden from the others until I return?"

She hesitated for a moment, her eyes fixated on him in the darkness. To him it seemed like the woman was trying to read him. But based on the way that she was looking at him he didn't think she could. Reluctantly, she nodded. "The home behind us, a friend from childhood lives there. He'll see us in, hide us. But what do you intend to do? Where are you going?"

"I need that bestiary," he whispered.

"So you're going to break into the chieftain's home and steal a book? That seems risky Marcus, even for a man as reckless as you."

"I appreciate the confidence," he said with a feigned smile. "But the book will be in Castron's saddlebags on his horse. He always keeps it there. Never known him to store it anywhere else. It's the only way I can stop it and free your daughter."

"Can't you just kill it?" she asked with a hint of optimism that was quickly squashed.

Marcus shook his head. "If I cause the Lesnik harm, it'll use that bark skin mark and your baby to heal itself. That's the purpose of the mark. It's a magical connection. As it grows weaker, it drains the life of the marked one to heal. So if I kill the beast, I'll have succeeded in making it kill your child so that it can live again."

She offered him no reply when he finished speaking. But he hadn't expected one. What was one to say when they had just been told that their young baby, who had done no wrong yet in her life, had been chosen as a sacrifice to an ancient forest beast which would kill her to keep itself strong and alive?

He cast a glance up towards the sky, watching for only a brief moment as the moon crept ever higher and he immediately felt himself getting antsy. He needed to get that book and try to end this before the sun arose on a new day. If the dawn came and went before he'd stopped the Lesnik's rampage, all of this would have been for naught. In the morning, the apothecary would condemn Kyia and the baby and he'd be forced to either let the villagers kill the baby to end the Lesnik's wrath or slaughter an entire village to save the woman. Neither option was appealing.

"I need you to go, get into the house and stay hidden until I come back," he told her quickly, hoping she would take his commands better than he had taken those of Castron and Piers. "If I'm not back before dawn, you need to leave. Take my horse and ride. Ride until you can't ride any longer and then go further still."

"But if you're not back..."

"Don't worry about me. Just take the baby and leave if I'm not back. If they kill me then that was to be my fate. A friend once told me that what's happened was meant to happen, and that is an expression of faith in the nature of the Creator. If ever there was a time to believe in those words, it would be now." He smiled at her. "Now go."

Kyia lingered there, hidden behind the bale of hay with him. Her eyes looked him over carefully. For a while he assumed that she was going to offer some protest or tell him why it was that she was not going to leave him as he commanded. She looked conflicted, lost in her own thoughts. And just when he thought she was going to do something rash and stupid to make him keep her with him, she did something far different.

She kissed him. It had taken him by surprise, her cold lips pressed tightly against his. But his surprise quickly turned to pleasure. He thought about letting the moment last forever. But the pleasure that her kiss had brought would be sullied forever if he did not find a way to save her baby from the Lesnik. If saving the child hadn't been reason enough to fight this hard to save her daughter, then the kiss gave him all the more reason he could ever need.

He pulled away from her and she muttered, "Go Marcus. Be careful."

He hesitated for a moment. But, without another word, he slank away from the hay bale where she had taken shelter. His mind, once so focused on how he was going to stop the Lesnik, had become clouded by the kiss that Kyia had given him. It was the first time that he'd been kissed in a very long time, since before he began his training as a Knight of the King. For some reason he could not stop thinking about it.

He needed to focus. Find the book. Read the book. Stop the Lesnik. Those could be his only thoughts if he was going to succeed.

Marcus lowered himself to a crouch and crept through the village on soft and nimble feet. He moved slowly, doing his best to keep all of his weight on the balls of his feet as he moved. He clung to the sides of buildings that were cloaked in shadow the way moss clung to the side of a tree. He tried to time his movements to the ambient sounds of the world around him. When he heard an owl's call in the dead of the night, he would scurry from place to place, using the sound to muffle and mask the sound of his footsteps upon the grass. He kept his head down to avoid anyone seeing his face.

Marcus was like a shadow in the night, moving from place to place without being seen. And once he reached the edge of town, he saw the chieftain's home before him, the wooden home that still filled his gut with rage.

Across from where he crouched, he could see Castron's horse still tied to the same hitching post the old man had placed her at earlier that day, though it now felt more to Marcus that a lifetime had passed. So much had happened, so much had changed in less than half a day that he could scarcely believe it.

All he needed to do was make it across the clearing to the horse and grab the book. It sounded so simple in his head. But nothing was ever as simple as it sounded. He knew that and yet he'd still allowed the simplicity of it all to trick his mind.

The clearing he needed to cross was bathed in moonlight, the pale glow of the heavenly orb casting everything before him in light. It wouldn't be too much of a problem if he was able to spring across the clearing without drawing the gaze of the two knights. If they saw him, things would get complicated very quickly. Making things worse, he didn't know where the commander and sword master were waiting. If they were in the home and happened to see him, they'd surely stop him. And if they were already outside patrolling the forests, they'd surely see him as he raced across a moonlit clearing.

He bushed the worries from his mind. He couldn't worry about that now. If the knights tried to stop him he would deal with that in the moment. But he did not have time to delay. He did not have the time to sit and think of how he would handle every scenario which might unfold as soon as he started to cross that clearing. He would have to do what the commander had told him all good knights must do, improvise when the first plan failed. And that's exactly what he would do.

Marcus sprinted across the clearing. His eyes bounced between Castron's horse, the forest to his left and the door. He watched carefully for signs of movement in the darkness. But he saw nothing.

As he approached the horse of the man who would've been his commander if he had just kept his wits about him and not done what he thought was right, a terrible thought occurred to him for the first time since he'd resolved to come here; *What if the book isn't in his saddle bag?*

The thought hadn't occurred to him until just now. He'd been so sure the commander would stow the bestiary in the saddle bags he'd committed to this mad scramble, and it could have all been for nothing.

But it was too late to turn back now. Kyia's baby did not have time for him to second guess his choices. She needed him to act. So he did.

Marcus continued to the commander's horse and dared to take a quick peek over his left shoulder. The knights still hadn't appeared. But he was still not safe until he was out of this clearing. His hands frantically grabbed for the flaps of the man's saddle bag, jerking it open as quickly as he possibly could and began to rummage around. Had he been a praying man he'd have sung the Creator every prayer he knew. The book was in there. The weathered bestiary was so easily distinguished just by the coarseness of the old tanned leather cover that he would've known it was the book even if he was blind.

He snatched the book and tucked it under his arm. He ducked in front of the horse and made himself as small as he could as he gave one last quick glance around the clearing to make sure that neither of the knights had appeared.

But still he saw no man in the clearing. So Marcus took a deep breath and readied himself. It was time to get his horse.

Marcus raced to the mare. If he tried to loosen the straps that he'd tied, he could not be sure that the mare would not whiny or neigh. If she did, someone would surely hear her. And that was not an option. So he drew steel, pulling a dagger he kept hidden in his waistline free from his belt and slashed the reins as close to the wooden column as possible. It'd be hard to control the horse but at least they wouldn't be able to catch him.

He grabbed the two splintered halves of the destroyed reins and gave the mare a quick tug, beckoning her to follow him. She didn't resist him, though he couldn't blame her for that. He wouldn't enjoy being tied to a post and forced to stand there for a long while.

The two of them broke into a run and they disappeared into the tree line without incidence. For a moment, he thought about thanking the Creator for letting him do such a thing without getting caught by the knights. But he decided against it. If the Creator helped him save this baby, maybe they'd have a little chat and he'd send up a prayer or two. Maybe.

He scampered into the darkness of the forest and allowed himself a moment of rest. He rubbed the side of the mare's head gently and reached into the saddle bag upon the horse's back. He pulled a few wild carrots he'd spotted growing in the forests not far from the fortress of the knights from the saddle bags and offered them to the mare. She whinnied in what he hoped was happiness as she took the carrots from him and crunched on them as he rubbed her sides.

He wished he could take her with him where he was planning to go. But there was no way he could take her into the village without being caught. He dumped some more carrots from the saddlebag onto the forest floor, hoping it would be enough to keep her in place long enough for him to retreat to Kyia's house and read the bestiary on Lesniks.

He slank back towards the village, keeping himself confined to the outskirts as he quickly made his way around the outside of the village to the last house, to the house where he'd destroyed any chance of having the future he'd long dreamed of having.

He slipped quietly inside, pushing the door closed as best as he could and strode across the floor of the home to the far wall where one of the braziers still burned with fire. He grabbed the worn brazier and made his way quickly to the table. As he passed the bookshelf, he caught sight of the woodcutter's axe that had once belonged to Kyia's husband. The tool gave him all the resolve he needed to continue on. The man was no longer around to defend his wife and daughter. So Marcus would do it in his stead.

He set the old book down and opened it carefully, not wanting to see what further wrath he would draw from Castron if he also tore one of the yellowed pages of the ancient book. He skimmed the pages as quickly as his eyes would allow him to, using the crudely drawn pictures of the beasts in question and the names atop the pages to quickly dismiss them as not the one that he was searching for.

Page after page flipped by and still he did not see anything about the Lesnik. Goblins, trolls and banshees. Dragons, drakes and basilisks. Even Fire Demons, Reavers and Ice Giants had pages in the book, all three of them beings thought to exist only in legends and fairytales. But no Lesniks. At least, not that he'd found yet.

Eventually, he did find the beast in the book, though he nearly passed it by when he saw that there was no crude drawing of the beast amidst the brief paragraphs that discussed the beast and how to best it. He read the words on the page quickly.

*A*MONG THE MOST *territorial of beasts, the Lesnik is known to prowl the forests around the home of the one who wears the bark skin mark from which it draws strength and power in times of great need. The only guaranteed way to ward the beast off is to kill the one who possesses the bark skin mark from which it draws this strength. This seems to sever the link between the beast and man, causing it to return to the depths of the forest from which it came.*

However, there exist unconfirmed rumors of other ways to drive the beast away from the settlements of men. Some Elvish villagers claim to have driven the beast off by transferring the bark skin mark from one man to another through a bizarre blood letting ritual. By shedding blood upon the mark, it was transferred from one man to another on his death bed and when the old man died, so too did the Lesnik. Or at the very least, ceased its attacks upon the villages.

Others claim that they were able to best the creature by seeking out its lair in the deep of the forest and driving it away with a show of force. If the beast feels threatened in its own lair, which is often made near large forest clearings for reasons we do not yet understand, it flees into the forest's heart and with that, the bark skin mark will vanish from the one afflicted by it.

Other ways, such as magic and curses, have since been debunked. When in doubt, kill the bearer of the bark skin mark. Or leave the beast alone entirely. But do not, under any circumstances, attack the beast with intent to kill. Not only will you achieve nothing but you'll also find yourself amongst the dead.

WHEN HE FINISHED READING, he felt a smile crease the corner of his mouth and a wave of optimism came over him quickly. There was still a chance he could save the baby. No matter how slight it was... It was still a chance.

Though he would've liked to have done the safer of the methods and transferred the bark skin mark to another, he knew there were no others who would willingly accept the mark knowing that it would mean their death. He would've done it himself, undertaken that burden from the young girl if he knew he could count on the others to do what it took to protect the babe if his death did not stop the beast in the forest. But he had no way to be sure. If they drove a blade through his chest and the beast continued the attacks on the village... He didn't even want to think of that. He would not waste this night on something that could prove futile.

He had only one choice in all this. There was only one way to try to end the Lesnik's reign of terror. He wished in that moment that his resolve was stronger, his courage unwavering as Castron's always seemed to be. He wished that he did not feel a massive hole of dread and despair deep in his gut. He wished that there was not a lump in his throat that did not seem like it would cease anytime soon. But above all else, he wished he could ask Piers and Castron for their aid. The three of them doing what he was about to undertake alone would have been far less risky. With the two knights aiding him, his chances of making it back to the village would be much greater.

But Marcus was no fool. No aid would come from Castron. And because of that, Piers would be unable to help him. If he was to do this, he was going to do it alone.

His legs began to tremble with nerves at the thought of doing what he knew he needed to do. He struggled to steady himself but found that the trembling and shaking legs would not be easily stilled. So he lowered himself into the dusty chair the woman had offered him before all this chaos had started and tried to calm himself.

His mind began to wander, thinking of all the risks he was going to take by doing this. Risks he was doing for a woman that he'd just met and the baby girl which did not belong to him. He was going to die for a stranger in the dark forest, cold and alone, his heroic sacrifice quickly forgotten by all but a few. The memory of Elesia was short and it would not be long before Marcus was all but forgotten by these lands. It was not the legacy he'd always dreamed he'd leave. And it was most assuredly not the way that he imagined he'd die.

As his mind wandered, so too did his eyes. They examined the small home in its softly lit orange glow. They moved all about the room, sparsely taking in the details of Kyia's dwelling when they fell onto something and did not stray from it.

It was the baby's crib. It lay on its side, clearly having been toppled over in the struggle between him and the commander. But he could hardly remember when it may have happened in the chaos that had erupted. The wood looked to have splintered and cracked and he wasn't sure why, but it upset him greatly. It was a crib unfit for the young girl to lie in anymore, a crib she'd never get to lie in again if he failed.

It was all the resolve he needed. A broken crib should not have given him strength or courage that night. Yet it had. It had shown him what he was fighting so hard to protect. It had shown him why the commander was wrong for wanting to kill the young babe. It made him remember his purpose. It made him remember his oath.

Marcus rose to his feet, his courage compelling him to do so. He turned to the bookshelf and grabbed hold of the woodcutter's axe which rested within it. He hesitated for a moment, not wanting to take the axe. It was the last memory Kyia had of her husband. But it was also the thing that would save her daughter. His sword would not cut through tree limbs and vines. But that axe would.

He decided that if Kyia took offense with him for doing it, he'd ask her forgiveness later. But saving her daughter was all that mattered to him now. He took the axe in hand, lit a single torch from the woman's brazier and left the home, heading back out into the brisk night air.

He walked brazenly through the village, doing little to conceal his movements in the shadows as he had before. If the villagers saw him, it no longer mattered. He'd either come back from this a hero or he wouldn't come back at all. He followed along the paths of worn grass until he saw the spot in the forest where he'd left the mare.

He crossed into the forest and to his relief the mare was still standing in the same spot where he'd left her, as if she was still waiting for him. He grabbed hold of her saddle and hoisted himself onto her back. He settled in quickly and gave the horse a few gentle pats on the side of her neck. He rubbed her with as much affection as he could.

"This could be our last ride together girl," he muttered weakly, talking more to himself than to the horse. "Lets make it worth something." The words surprisingly made him feel better though he couldn't be sure why they did. Marcus sighed heavily and told himself he was doing the right thing. This was how he kept his oath. This is how he'd become an Oathkeeper.

He took the tattered remains of the horse's reigns and ushered her onwards, heading deeper into the dark heart of the forest, intent to find the Lesnik's lair and drive it from these lands, or to die trying.

CHAPTER 6

Marcus found the twisted bodies of the villagers with relative ease. How he'd managed to do it in the darkness of the forest with only the slowly dimming flames of the torch he'd brought with him, he had no idea. But he'd somehow led the mare through the forest exactly to the spot.

The Lesnik, surprisingly, hadn't stalked him for any of the ride. Nor had he even seen the thing, though in the darkness it was nearly impossible to tell. The long shadows that the trees gave off, even in this place where the moon's light could barely break the canopy of leaf and limb that lingered above, seemed to dance as he looked at them, ever changing and shifting as if they were playing tricks on his mind. The darkness that surrounded him was not merely the absence of light. It was a thick layer of blackness which obscured everything which fell outside the slowly shrinking circle of orange fire which surrounded him.

The shadows were nothing compared to the silence however. He'd been unnerved by it during the day. But at night, everything seemed to be much worse. He could not see what lurked out in the dark. If he could not see nor hear it then he could easily be taken by surprise. Vigilance was the way to survive. When a man loses focus his chances of death rise drastically.

But there was no way that he could be vigilant when all he

could see was nothing. A bear or pack of wolves could've lingered just beyond the edge of his light. And because they did not seem keen to make a sound, he could easily stumble upon them without ever knowing that they were right there, awaiting him.

He gave the mare a nudge and she continued deeper into the forest. Of all the things that seemed to have gone wrong today the one thing that hadn't disappointed him at all was the horse. No matter where he tried to make her go, she went. She could not have felt good about going into these eerie woods. Yet she'd willingly done it without as much as a neigh or whinny. She just galloped when he wanted her to and cantered along when he didn't. Marcus had never been overly fond of horses. He thought them to be things you got attached to and then it would be killed in battle. But the mare that he sat upon had grown on him. He'd ride upon her back anywhere.

The horse and rider traveled deeper into the dark wood as a gentle snow began to fall from the sky, blanketing his gambeson in a powdery white fluff. Worst of all, the snow caused the last light of his torch to flicker out of existence. The rider grumbled to himself in frustration and threw the smoldering torch into the darkness. It was useless now.

The only thing worse than the darkness was the cold wind howling through the trees, making them rustle like living things in the darkness. It was bitterly cold, even in his gambeson. The cold nibbled at his cold skin, sending violent shivers down his back and making him long for warmth. If he didn't freeze to death before the night was over, it was probably a miracle.

The closer to the heart of the forest they seemed to get, the worse things in the forest seemed to become. The air felt heavier, the blackness more oppressive, and everything seemed to feel warmer. Marcus was not sure if it was his own mind imagining those things or if something else entirely was happening. Perhaps he felt warmer because no air could find a way to blow through the densely packed mammoth trees which blocked his view in every direction. Perhaps the darkness felt more oppressive because the moon had been entirely blocked from his view by the canopy. Perhaps the air felt heavier because something was making it that way.

Or, more likely, he was beginning to panic. With each thunderous step that the mare took, he moved a step closer to the thing which could easily bring about his death. A thing which he could not kill nor cause harm to without fear of what it might do to Kyia's daughter to heal the damage he'd inflict upon it.

Making everything worse, he knew the beast was out there stalking these woods. It had followed him as they moved earlier. He had every reason to believe that even though he could not see it, the Lesnik was still following close behind him, stalking him the way a hunter stalks its prey. He had wandered into the beast's home, into its territory. In here the rules of men and the Knights of the King meant nothing. The beast would not fight fair and it would not stop its assault once it began until he was dead.

Marcus had every right to be panicking. Only a fool would not be nervous by what he was about to do. But the difference between a man and a knight was that the knight would continue on deeper and deeper into the woods regardless of how much his brain told him to retreat. Even though he knew Castron would never make him a knight now, he knew Marcus the man would not be able to save Kyia's daughter. But Marcus the knight could.

He rode further, not allowing his fears to overcome him. He passed through small streams of gently rippling waters. The mare leapt over fallen trees and across dried up creek beds. She cantered over small hills and through strange archways made by fallen trees and dirt. No matter how far he beckoned the mare to go, the horse did it without fear.

Something caught his eye ahead. Something so strange and unusual in these dark and oppressive woods he gave the reins a quick tug and stopped the horse. It wasn't the Lesnik or any other creature before him. Nor was it more of the twisted roots entwined with more bodies.

Ahead of him Marcus saw a large clearing basked in the soft pale glow of the moon. In any other forest he'd have thought nothing of it and carried on riding. Amidst these dark trees a moonlit clearing was about the strangest thing he could expect to see. But it was also the best thing he could have hoped to see.

Lesniks were said to make their lairs near clearings. The teachings were not quite sure why that was. But the generally accepted belief was that they did it so that they would have easy access to the sunlight. They rationalized that Lesniks needed sunlight to grow just as trees did. Whether it was true or not, no one really knew. But they believed it to be true. That was enough for him.

Marcus grumbled to himself and gave the mare a few delicate pats on the side of the neck. It was the best he could do to thank her for bringing him this far. This had been the only clearing he'd managed to find in all his travels. If the beast truly did have a lair, it was nearby. And if it didn't, he likely die from the bite of the cold long before he found it in this forest.

Marcus climbed down out of the saddle and tossed the last of the carrots from his saddlebag to the forest floor at the mare's feet. He thought about tying her off to one of the trees for a moment but quickly decided against it. If the Lesnik killed him, the horse would be trapped here to starve to death or be ravaged by beasts, unable to move from the tree or defend herself. He'd not leave her to that fate. So he took his chances and hoped she'd remain near as she had the first time he'd left her.

He treaded carefully as he walked across the uneven forest floor, his eyes darting back and forth quickly as he approached the clearing basked in the warm and welcoming light of the moon. He clambered gently over gnarled tree roots which nearly tripped him in the darkness. He ducked beneath fallen trees and skillfully evaded a patch of forest floor littered with skeletal remains of various animals that had been broken and snapped. Falling into it surely would've seen him impaled. But he took it as a good sign. This had to be the Lesnik's doing.

The darkness of the forest around him was almost as chilling as the brisk night air. With each step he took the moonlight illuminated the cool mist which escaped his mouth after each breath or grunt. The snow seemed to be falling faster too, creating this odd effect of whiteness and light where he knew there was only darkness. The snowflakes seemed to coalesce into a puffy blanket of white upon the blunted head of the woodcutter's axe he now carried in his hand. As annoying as the cold watery drops of snow were, he was almost thankful for them. They made it seem like it was brighter in the forest than it truly was. Just thinking it was lighter was enough to help put his weary and fearful heart at rest if only briefly.

When he finally stepped into the clearing, the first thing he could think to do was look up. He watched as the snowflakes descended from the heavens upon him, felt their coldness land upon his face. It was stupid, he knew, but he stuck his tongue out and tried to catch some of the snowflakes in his mouth. For the first time in a great many moons, he felt like a child again, playing in the forests during a snowfall, catching snowflakes in his mouth.

But as quickly as he allowed his memories of childhood to come to him, he pushed them aside. He had a monster to stop. If he didn't, then there was a young girl who would never get to experience the childhood which he had.

Marcus refocused. He allowed his eyes to scan the forest around him. He didn't know what one of the beast's lairs might look like. But he suspected that he would know it when he saw it. Or at least, he hoped he'd know it when he saw it. He wasn't overly familiar with what a 'lair' might look like. Nor was he particularly certain what might differentiate a tree monster's lair from every other tree in a forest full of trees. But he needed to find it.

Marcus saw something just beyond the clearing's edge. A number of pillars of gnarled and twisted roots rose high towards the treetops which all seemed to be connected together by creeping ivy and flower bearing vines. It looked almost as if it formed a tunnel heading deeper into the forest. It was the oddest thing Marcus had ever seen. It was connected to the Lesnik some-how. It had to be.

He crossed the clearing slowly, his eyes darting from side to side. If this truly was the beast's lair then it would surely try to defend it. He searched for a towering shadow. He listened for a strange roar or screech or something which might have belonged to a monstrous beast of these woods. But when he saw nothing, heard nothing, he quickened his pace.

Marcus made his way towards the nearest pillar of twisted roots. He tightened his grip on the woodcutter's axe in his hands. They said the Lesnik was awakened and became hostile when man attacked the trees, destroying the forests where they resided. So how would the beast react to him attacking the trees and roots where it made its lair?

He was about to find out.

Marcus took one last deep breath to try to strengthen his wavering resolve. As soon as he started there was no turning back. The beast would come for him and he'd be forced to fight it. This could be the last moment of his life.

A thousand thoughts raced across his mind. Memories of his youth, his mother and father laughing with him, his friends Kan and Gerald racing up the side of a volcano with their mother's old rings to be cast into the fires of the mountain. He thought of his training with the knights, of beating Piers and earning the admiration of Castron. And then he thought of Kyia and her daughter hiding behind hay barrels, fearful for their lives because of a beast.

Marcus drew back the axe and slammed the blunted head into the pillar of roots. The edge, though blunted and dulled and nicked, left a large gash in the pillar which seemed to weep amber colored sap much the way a wound would weep with blood. He struck the spot again and again, refusing to stop until the beast either attacked him or he cut all the way through the pillar.

His breathing had become labored and the axe, heavy in his hands by the time he gave one last forceful swing, nearly splitting the pillar of roots in two. A single root, by his guess, was all that held the pillar together. One more swing and the pillar would topple, taking the entire tunnel structure down with it. He drew back the axe and prepared to swing.

But the swing never came.

The earth beneath his feet began to shake and a low grating

moan pierced the silence of the forest. The trees around him began to rustle and move in the darkness. And from the deep of the woods, charging through the tunnel of ivy and vines, came the Lesnik.

It looked like a massive gangly man in the darkness. But as it drew closer to him, he began to see the finer details of the massive monster that raced towards him on two long, spindly legs that looked to be made of tree limbs that were entangled and entwined. The rest of its body appeared to be made from the same twisted limbs and roots which made up its legs. The hands of the beast came to long, jagged points. Most of the beast's body was covered in thick green moss and algae which caused the thing to look like something that had crawled out of a swamp. The head of the beast was hidden behind the decaying skull of some long dead forest creature with numerous antlers sprouting from it. But its piercing red eyes were visible in the darkness of the night, perhaps even more so because of the white snow falling around them.

The beast towered over him. But it was not swift of foot. If it had been it would've trampled him while he was standing there dumbfounded, staring at the massive forest devil. He'd not known what to expect a Lesnik to look like. But it wasn't that.

Marcus was able to lunge to the side as the beast trampled into the clearing, the long gangly arms swinging back and forth near the ground as it moved. Marcus spun quickly and chased the beast into the clearing. At least there he wouldn't have to contend with the trees.

The Lesnik stopped and threw its head back. The creature bellowed a deafening roar which carried on the still of the night. Standing amidst the clearing it was the most horrifying thing that he'd ever seen. In the pale light of the moon every detail about the creature seemed to become more terrifying. The roots of the beast's body seemed to glisten with fresh blood. A number of weapons were lodged in its body, broken swords and pikes and spear shafts which had long since rusted and become coated in the green algae. Barbs and sticks protruded from the beast's body like the quills of a porcupine.

But still Marcus charged the beast. In the heat of the moment ,with a surge of adrenaline overcoming him, he raced towards the beast and drove the axe into the back of one of the beast's spindly legs.

A mistake. He wasn't supposed to harm the beast, only scare it. He was supposed to make it fear man and that was all. Harming the beast meant it would harm the young girl to heal itself. He was angry with himself for doing something so stupid. He would've scolded himself in that moment for being so stupid but he had other things to occupy his mind.

The Lesnik bellowed in pain. Marcus barely had time to free the head of his axe from the beast's wooden leg before roots began to erupt from the snow covered ground, moving at him like a wave upon the water's surface. He rolled quickly to the side as the wave of roots surged passed him and disappeared into the trees.

Marcus had only risen to his feet before the towering forest demon was upon him, those gangly sharp claws swiping viciously through the air. He somehow managed to evade the strikes. But more came at him, each as quick and vicious as the one before it.

If he'd have been even a step slower, he'd surely have been torn to pieces by the frenzied and vicious strikes of the Lesnik. He ducked and weaved and rolled seemingly constantly, never really able to find a way to mount any kind of counterattack. The beast was overwhelming him.

That was the exact opposite of what he'd planned on happening. He'd hoped to overwhelm the beast with his attacks, perhaps make it fear that it could be killed by those who dwelled within the forest and make it flee these lands in search of another forest to protect. He was supposed to be the one attacking it, making it feel fear. Not the other way around.

He found himself dodging a nearly constant stream of swinging claws that very easily could rend the flesh from his bones. With each claw that barely missed splitting him in two, his mind began to think a little more about the possibility of attacking the creature with the axe. If he could sever one of the beast's hands, he would stand a better chance of surviving.

But if he did that then he would only be causing the young girl further harm. If he severed one of the Lesnik's hands, he would be choosing his own safety over the safety of the baby. For that he felt ashamed. He'd rebuked Castron a number of times because the man sought to choose the safety of the village over the safety of the baby. He'd come to blows with the man over that argument. But now, as he fought for his life, he was thinking about letting the baby come to harm so that he could survive the fight with the beast.

In that moment, Marcus was no better than the commander he'd quarreled with. He would not allow himself to stoop to that. His life was not worth more than the safety of the baby.

He continued his evasive maneuvers, spinning and rolling away from the beast's strikes with quickness that could not be taught. But he didn't know how much longer he could keep up the effort. Fatigue was beginning to set in. His legs were getting heavier with each frantic scramble across the clearing to evade another strike. His lungs were burning from the shallow breaths of cold air he was forced to draw in. The snowflakes landing on his exposed skin made it feel even colder than it was. If the fight continued much longer, he was going to die, either from the claws of the Lesnik or his lungs bursting from the cold air and filling with blood.

He managed to dodge a few more blows but his swiftness was waning quickly. He rolled to evade a strike and felt the jagged tip of one of the beast's claws rip through his chainmail. He felt warm, sticky blood forming on his upper arm. But the beast did not give him time to assess the wound before another attack came. This one ripped into his leg, slashing through his trousers and leaving a horrid gash on his lower leg. He limped for a moment, fighting back the pain. But another strike came. The rush of adrenaline took over and he managed to evade it. The pain in his leg subsided. But he knew it was only temporary.

The beast swung again. This time it had caught him flat footed. There was no dodging or rolling away from the sharp claws that were hurtling towards him. There was only one option now aside from death. It was an option he despised. But he had no other choice. The beast would kill him if he did nothing.

Marcus drew back the woodcutter's axe and slammed it upwards toward's the beasts chest, knowing that it was his only chance at stopping the coming blow. He watched as the head of the axe embedded itself in the Lesnik's upper chest. The creature stopped abruptly, a few severed tree limbs falling free from its body and disturbing the layer of fresh snow which covered the earth below his feet. That was what he'd hoped would happen. He needed the beast to stop its frenzied charge.

The Lesnik reared back and roared towards the heavens once more. Luckily, it did not appear to be harmed or perturbed by the axe he'd just lodged in its torso. But there was something else he now had to contend with. He'd lost the only weapon he had other than his useless sword. And it did not appear he'd managed to do anything to drive it away from these lands. All he'd done was make it angry.

Marcus had failed.

His legs were heavy, too heavy to support his weight. His head felt light. His arm throbbed. The gash in his leg was bleeding too much. Everything hurt. This was to be his death. He was absolutely sure of that.

His legs buckled and he collapsed in a heap on the snow covered forest floor. His head rolled to the side and he saw that the blood from his leg was already turning the snow a crimson red color. When he coughed, his spit was filled with blood and he could feel more blood running down his throat, gagging him.

Marcus was dying.

His eyesight was obscured by the white snow falling from the sky. He struggled to keep his eyelids open as pain and blood loss threatened to claim his consciousness. He watched through half seeing eyes as the Lesnik moved towards him. The beast was even more massive as he lay on the ground, a gangly beast large enough to block the entire moon from his view. The tree monster was like a giant he'd heard about in stories of old. It looked to reach the sky in his hazy vision.

One moment, the beast was there, standing above him as his vision faded to darkness. When he next opened his eyes, the world was enveloped in bright orange light. A giant ball of flames lurked above him, casting everything that he could see in an orange glow that immediately made him think of the rising sun.

Was it the sunrise? Had he been lying in the snow, dying, all night long? It didn't seem possible. But the glowing orange light above his head seemed to say otherwise, that somehow, he'd been lying in the snow all night, waiting for the dawn of a new day to greet him as he succumbed to his wounds.

Then, he saw the grizzled face of Piers right above him. In his hand he held a torch which glowed with the bright orange light he'd seen the world drowned in just moments before. He watched silently as the man took a cloth dressing and, after packing the wound full of snow, wrapped it tightly around the gash in his leg. Marcus was surprised that the wound did not pain him as the man touched it.

Piers produced a small vial of something from a small pouch on his belt and poured some of it down his throat. The taste was horrible even in his half conscious state. The liquid burned going down his throat. But it was nothing compared to the horrible sensation it caused in his stomach. His gut lurched and for a moment he felt like he was going to puke. But the nausea and burning passed. And when they did, Marcus found he had the strength to sit up.

"Easy now kid," Piers cautioned as he put a hand on Marcus' shoulder to steady him as he rose to a seated position. "That tonic is not for the faint of heart. Seen good men puke after drinking this stuff. So take it slow."

"What is that?" Marcus asked with a raspy and hoarse voice.

"You live long enough, someday I might tell you," the sword master said bluntly as he began to study the gash in his upper arm. "The leg needs stitching or you'll bleed to death. The arm isn't as bad. Thank the Creator it's not your sword arm. But still, it could do with stitching. Might I ask what it was you were thinking?"

Marcus grunted in pain as he felt the knight pack the wound on his arm with snow and then begin to wrap the dressing around it. "I stole the bestiary from Castron's saddle and read it. It claimed that a Lesnik could be driven away from the lands it inhabited. So I had hoped..."

"You thought that confronting an ancient forest devil with a sword and an axe would be enough to drive it away from lands it has lived in for thousands of years?" the knight asked with a smirk. The smirk quickly gave way to a delighted laugh. "I do not yet know if I should admire you for being so brave or scold you for being so foolish. The beast does not fear man. It will never fear man. Men are fleeting things. We come and go. But that beast is eternal. So long as there are trees in this world, the Lesnik will never truly die. So there was no way you could've driven it away from these lands. Not like that."

"At least I tried something instead of just accepting that we needed to kill a baby." The words had come out more harsh and accusatory than he'd intended them to. At first he was afraid he'd offended the sword master who had saved his life just moments before. But if Piers minded his words, he did not act like it. Nor did he even acknowledge them. "She doesn't deserve to die for the chieftain's sins. Castron can say what he wants, but he's wrong. This is the chieftain's fault and Castron is defending him."

"You seem quick to pass blame onto other men," Piers noted. "Yet you do not pass blame on yourself. You claim them to be wrong, but you say nothing about your mistakes. You attacked this beast when it's done nothing to you, just as Castron wishes to kill the girl when she's done nothing to him. So how are you any better than the commander?"

"She's a baby," Marcus replied angrily. "And it's a monster."

"It is not a monster just because men claim it to be," Piers remarked. "The Lesnik is the protector of the forests. It does not do the things it does out of malice. The beast attacks to defend itself and the forests around it. Yet you rode into its lair and provoked it to attack you. Seems to me that you were the real monster. You came seeking blood and the beast defended itself."

Marcus could only sigh as he listened to the words of the sword master. He hadn't yet thought about that, but Piers was right. He'd rode out into the forest with the intent of driving the beast away from these trees, seeking blood. He had been the monster attacking the Lesnik in its home. He was the beast that came to kill it in the middle of the night. Marcus was the monster. Just as Castron was the monster that wanted to kill the babe. They were both wrong.

"Maybe I'm not better than Castron," Marcus grumbled. "Maybe we're both the monsters plaguing this village. But if I was wrong to attack the Lesnik and he is wrong to kill the babe, there must be another way. Because I cannot allow any harm to come to the babe."

"I don't like it either Marcus. I wish there was another way to save the baby. But there just... isn't. The beast marked her. There is nothing else we can do to save the village. I argued with Castron, urged him to try to find another way. But the man would not relent. Though he was rather angry that a young knight in training had struck him."

"I don't regret what I did."

"Nor should you. You stood up for what you thought was right. That is to be admired. Castron would agree with such a thing. What you should regret is deciding to attack the man who would be your commander if you are to become a Knight of the King. He could execute you for that."

Marcus grimaced, the pain shooting through his body so consuming that it was the only thought that he could focus on in that moment. "That why you're here? Make sure the beast doesn't kill me before Castron gets the chance to."

The sword master shook his head. "I saw you approach the chieftain's home. Then I saw you riding out into the forest and wondered what you were doing. I'd no intentions of coming out here to find you. Figured I'd let you survive or die on your own. Prove your strength to Castron. But the apothecary came to

Castron not long ago. He told the commander where to find Kyia and the baby. I think they mean to kill the baby tonight. And I cannot stop them on my own. I need help. And you're the only man who can help."

"Stop them?" The words caught him by surprise. He hadn't expected Piers to defy the will of the commander. But if the man's words were true then that was exactly what he was planning to do. "You wish to go against Castron?" Piers nodded. "But that's treason. You can be hanged for that."

"I know. But I can't sit by and watch the commander kill a baby. There has to be some other way to stop all this from happening. So I had hoped to stall him for the moment until I could figure out if there even is another way."

"There is," Marcus croaked weakly as he mustered what strength he could find to rise to his feet before Piers forced him back down, urging him to remain sitting for now. "According to the bestiary, we can transfer the bark skin mark from the baby to a willing victim. It's a legend that the ancient knights were not sure worked. But it's worth a try if it saves the babe's life."

Piers scoffed loudly. "You think anyone is foolish enough to accept that mark willingly when they know that it means they'll be put to death? How does one even transfer a mark? In some kind of rain dance?" His final words felt like they were intended to mock Marcus. But the young man did not allow the words to dissuade him.

"The bark skin mark is a magical binding, is it not?" Marcus asked the sword master quickly. "It serves to bind the Lesnik and the one afflicted by the mark, correct?" The knight sat and pondered for a moment as he continued wrapping the wound the beast had struck upon him. Eventually he shrugged and nodded. "It's akin to a curse then. And the bestiary mentioned that it was a blood-letting ritual and mentioned elves were involved with the alleged transferring. So why can we not transfer the mark in a blood ritual as the elves of ancient times did for curses."

"A blood ritual?" Piers asked dismissively. He seemed ready to argue with Marcus on the point. But when the young man said nothing, the knight began to think. He worked silently on the wrapping upon his leg, adjusting what had come loose when he'd tried to stand. When he finally finished, he turned to Marcus and said "That... is brilliant. A blood ritual could actually work. Do you know the words for the ritual?" Surprisingly, he did. Marcus had read enough about the ancient elves and their curse breaking rituals to have memorized the words. "But the victim that takes it must be willing to do so," the sword master cautioned again.

"Don't worry about that," Marcus replied shortly. He'd no intention of telling the sword master that if there was nobody who would take the mark from the babe then he would do it himself. If it meant that Kyia's baby got to live then he would willingly take the burden on.

The sword master's eyes had become narrow slits. Marcus knew the look. The man often looked like that when he was trying to determine what someone was hiding from him or trying to see through a lie. When a trainee seemed a little sloppy and tipsy during sparring practice and the sword master asked them if they'd had too much to drink, they'd always say they hadn't. And the sword master would look at them as he looked at Marcus now. The look made most men training under him nervous. But not Marcus. He kept his wits about him and refused to tell the man anything. "We've only one problem to contend with then," Piers muttered.

Castron. Marcus had been so concerned about convincing the sword master to help him that he'd forgotten about the commander. The man surely wouldn't allow them to try an unproven method on the babe. Not when the safety of the town was on the line. And he doubted that the apothecary would be willing to stand down either.

"We can't let Castron stop us," Marcus said as he staggered to his feet. He winced in pain and nearly cried out because of the pain that radiated from the gash in his leg. It throbbed under his weight. But he willed himself on. He was not going to let Kyia's babe die. Not while he still drew breath.

"I cannot cause any harm to my commander."

"I'm not asking you to. You keep the apothecary at bay. I'll deal with Castron."

"He'll not like that," Piers warned.

"I'll tell him he can hang me for treason in the morning if he doesn't like it then. Just handle the apothecary and let me deal with Castron." Marcus did not wait for the sword master to offer protest or tell him why he thought it to be a bad idea. He merely limped into the dark forest, intent to ride his horse hard back into town and confront the man who might have been his commander had he been a lesser man.

hen he could finally make out the faint shapes of the small huts of the village through the trees, Marcus nearly sighed with relief. The swirling snow was more akin to a blizzard now. But the snowfall did not bother Marcus. The biting cold did. Every man he'd ever met hated the snow, claimed it to be the thing which could take a man by surprise and kill him faster than a frenzied Banshee.

But Marcus knew that they mistook that for the cold. The cold was a quiet killer. It snuck up on unsuspecting men faster than the best assassin he'd ever seen. Then the cold burned while a man he tried to warm himself. But once the burning cold got inside you, it was too late. The cold was going to kill you. Somewhat luckily for the knight, he was sure that if he died of something this night, it wasn't going to be the cold.

His cloak kept him as warm as it could be expected to with the snow making it cold and wet. Snow covered his hair, making the shaggy black locks of hair atop his head look as white as Castron's. As it melted, the water dripped down on his neck and made him shiver. But that was nothing compared to the howling wind. It sliced through his wet clothes and gambeson like sharp daggers made of ice. The limbs of trees swayed and bounced in the driving winds, whacking the two men as they'd rode through the dark wood as quickly as their horses could take them in the perilous weather.

With each galloping step the horse took, searing pain shot up through his leg. He tried to focus on something else. The babe, the woodcutter's axe he'd lost in the chaos, Kyia's kiss. He even tried to focus on the burning of the cold. But none of it could distract him from the pain. Once he'd willed himself to look at the leg as it bounced in the stirrup as the mare raced amongst the trees. But when he saw that the cloth wrap was soaked in crimson blood and seemed to be getting wetter with each passing moment, he looked away and decided not to look at it again.

He followed after Piers as the man navigated his horse through the cleared lands on the outskirts of town, then into the town. As he rode through the gaps between the houses, he began to notice strange things seemed to have occurred in the town since he'd left. Vines and roots had erupted from the ground and begun to snake their way over most of the small huts. It was almost like nature was trying to reclaim the homes for itself. As they rode, they had to cut away the low hanging vines that draped between the houses to open their paths forward.

Marcus felt a pang of guilt at the sight of the vines and roots that covered most of the small huts in the village and snaked across the ground. The Lesnik was assailing their town because of him. He'd brought its wrath down upon them because he'd been unwilling to sacrifice one to save all the others. It was a sign of a bad knight that he couldn't bring himself to let one die to save many. Yet it was exactly the kind of man his mother would've been proud of.

As soon as he spotted the house with the hay bales that Kyia had been hiding behind, he heard the sharp yell of Kyia sound from within it. Marcus tugged the reins of the horse and slid out of the mare's saddle before she'd even stopped galloping. The wound upon his leg seemed to erupt with pain as soon as his feet hammered into the hard ground. But he disregarded the pain. He raced towards the door with a quickly worsening limp. He drew the sword from the scabbard at his side and cut away the vines that had started to cover the wooden door into the hut. He hacked and cleaved wildly.

As soon as he'd cut the vines away enough to squeeze through, he threw himself against the door. The door flew open and he charged inside.

The inside of the hut was furnished in much the same way as Kyia's. Only it was devoid of some of the pleasantries the woman had enjoyed such as the large table and bookshelves. It was also in the same state of disrepair as Kyia's house had been the last time he'd been inside it. The interior was ransacked and destroyed. Items lay strewn about, overturned and broken as though a great struggle had broken out only recently.

Opposite the door with his back to him, Marcus could see the old knight descending on Kyia and her baby as she tried to back away from the man. She was pleading with him to find another way. To his left, the broken beak nosed mask of the apothecary. The bird nosed man was struggling to restrain a man that Marcus hadn't seen before. Tall and broad, the man was thrashing wildly, shaggy yellow hair whipping violently from side to side as he tried to break free of the apothecary's grasp. His eyes were fixated on Kyia. He pleaded and begged the commander to leave her alone. But his words fell on deaf ears.

Marcus scurried across the floor as fast as his battered leg would carry him. He paid the apothecary no mind. Piers would handle him. His only concern was getting the commander to stand down.

As Marcus closed in on the old man the old knight turned to look at him. His sword was already in hand. Before Castron could even realize what was happening, Marcus brought his sword down quickly in an overhead strike. Their blades collided with a thunderous *clang* and the sword of Castron fell from the man's unprepared grasp. One moment they heard the blade hit the floor. The next, the tip of Marcus' sword was leveled towards the old knight's throat.

He heard a minor scuffle behind him. When he allowed himself to take a cautious glance, he saw Piers standing above the apothecary as the man lay on the floor cowering beneath the tip of the sword master's blade.

"What is the meaning of this?!" the old commander barked, enraged. His rage filled eyes looked first to Marcus. But when they made their way over to the sword master, they became violent and hate filled. The old man was nearly ready to erupt. But Marcus had gone too far to back down now. "Creator damn you, Piers. What in the bloody hell do you think yer doing?" The sword master did not offer him an answer. "This is treason," the old commander spat.

"You can hang me come the morning if you'd like," Marcus replied with a coldness that made the night air seem warm. He motioned for the commander to move away from the girl and the old man begrudgingly did so with the point of a sword hovering near his throat. His hateful eyes were menacing. But his evil glare was no match for Marcus' blade. "But the babe is not going to die."

Castron scoffed. "Then you bring doom upon this town. You refuse to kill a single baby and condemn the rest of these people to die." He raised his fingers and pointed out the open windows as vines crept across it, slowly blocking the moon's light and fresh snow from seeping into the house. "You did this, Marcus. This is your doing because you'll not kill a single babe."

"There's a way to do this without having to kill the child commander," Piers pleaded with the old man. "The bestiary..."

"I know damn well what the bestiary says," the commander interjected. "And it says that the only sure way to stop the beast is to kill the one that bears the bark skin mark upon their skin. So whatever method that the boy..."

Marcus pressed the tip of the blade against the commander's skin and he fell silent. "This boy has a fuckin' name. And this boy is going to save the baby. With or without your help."

The old man forced a stifled laugh, the point of Marcus' sword against his throat making him unwilling to move more than he had to. "And how do you reckon you're gonna do that?"

"Transfer the mark to a willing victim," came Marcus' answer.

His eyes strayed to Kyia. The woman was standing in the corner of the room with her daughter clutched tightly against her chest. Between them, acting like a barrier blocking a direct path towards her was the blonde man.

Castron laughed again. "An unproven method. How stupid..." Marcus pressed the blade deeper into the old man's skin. He fell silent for a moment in response and seemingly thought better of whatever he was going to say. After a long while the old man finally spoke again. "It's a legend boy, a story so baseless and unfounded that even the ancient and most knowledgeable Knights of the King were not able to decide if it was true or not. How would you even do it?"

"An Elvish Blood Ritual," Marcus replied shortly.

The old man looked at him and seemed ready to protest much the way Piers had when he'd first suggested it to him. But as quickly as the look of protest appeared upon his chiseled and angry face, it vanished. It was replaced by a look of quiet contemplation which lasted for what seemed like a long while. Then the contemplation became a look of begrudging respect and the old man looked to the sword master as he pressed a worn boot against the apothecary's chest to further still him. "Did you come up with that?" Piers merely shook his head.

Marcus was so focused on the commander that he was nearly completely caught off guard when he heard the voice of Kyia call out. "What is this ritual you speak of?"

Marcus turned. Kyia had stepped out from behind the man and was slowly approaching him as he held the commander at the point of his blade. She looked frightened clutching the small babe in her arms far tighter than she probably realized. But his words seemed to have given her a small glimmer of hope. Optimism hid behind her eyes, waiting to emerge. But she held it inside her, refusing to let it escape in case Marcus' plan did not work.

"It's an ancient ritual that the elves used to do in order to break curses that had been placed on one of their kind. They believed that a curse could be weakened by sharing it amongst more than one person. They'd find someone willing to share the burden of the curse with them. Both of them would cut their skin open and the cursed one would allow some of their tainted blood to mix with the pure blood of the one who was willing to share the burden. Sometimes they'd even completely transfer the curse from one to another. Curse placed upon a baby that is transferred to a grown man likely won't have the same effects. They'll be lessened," Marcus recalled. He hoped that was everything that Castron had taught them about the ancient rituals of the first to inhabit the lands that they walked upon. When he looked at the commander, he gave a begrudging nod of respect.

She thought for a few moments in quiet contemplation. The wind howled ominously outside. The shutters banged and clanged against the wooden building. She looked down at her daughter and seemed to allow hope to overcome her. She allowed a smile to crinkle the corner of her mouth. "Blood can do that?" she asked timidly.

"There's power in blood m'lady," Castron answered. "Most believe that the power to use magic is in the blood. Curses can be broken by blood. Lineages can portend the rise of heroes. Blood was used by ancient men to learn how to heal the body. It was used to study a great many things. There is a mysterious power in blood."

"Then do it," she demanded without asking another question. She did not know what the ritual would entail. She did not know if they would have to do something dark and dangerous. All she knew was that it could save her daughter. That was enough. "Do the blood ritual."

"It's not quite that simple," came the gruff voice of Piers from somewhere behind him. "Blood rituals only work when the person willing to take on the burden willingly accepts it. Can't just spill the blood upon another and expect it to just work. The one accepting it must swear an oath to the old gods and the new. There's magic at work in these rituals."

Kyia looked to Marcus for reassurance. But the man could only give a weak shake of his head. "He's right. Someone must willingly accept the bark skin mark. They must accept a thing which will get them killed come morning."

"Then I'll accept it," the woman said without a moment's hesitation. Dread rose into Marcus' stomach and it felt like his throat had locked as he looked at the woman. "I'll take the bark skin mark if it means that my daughter will live. I'll do it."

Marcus swallowed hard. His throat failed him. He tried to utter a sentence. Tried to offer her some words of encouragement or argue. But the only word he was able to muster was "no". Even the word felt weird as it left his mouth, as if his dry mouth had forgotten how to form the word that had escaped his lips.

"You don't get to decide this," Kyia said with a hint of anger in her voice. "She is my daughter. And I'll do whatever I must do in order to protect her. You could never understand."

The man mustered what little strength he had left. His leg and arm were on fire, the pain radiating from both wounds so overwhelming that he could barely focus on anything but it. As he struggled to stay on his feet, he felt his eyelids growing heavy. He swayed in place and his outstretched arm holding his sword at the commander's throat trembled under the weight of the blade. But he was not going to allow his fear and dread to stop him from trying to talk Kyia out of it. And from offering to take the burden in her place.

Marcus found his voice and spoke. "If we allow you to take the curse, this will have all been for nothing. We save your daughter and condemn her to live the rest of her life without a mother? That isn't how this is supposed to work." A tear stung at the corner of his eye as he somberly added words that seemed to tear his heart in half. "A child should not have to grow up without a mother."

"My daughter will live for 200 summers or more if this ritual works," Kyia said. She was trying to be calming and strong. But Marcus could hear the obvious tremble of fear in her voice. "And I will only be a mother to her for 20 of those summers. Once she reaches 20 summers, she'll be a grown woman. She'll have no more need of me. If I'm to choose between her having to suffer

20 summers without a mother or her perishing to this accursed mark on her skin... I think you know there is only one right choice to make."

Marcus shook his head weakly. It was the only thing he could do to plead for her not to do this. He wanted to beg her not to do this. He wanted her to be beside her daughter as she grew old. The girl would need her. And he'd take her place if it meant the girl would be able to grow up with her mother at her side.

"Kyia," a deep voice he hadn't heard before said, a voice that he quickly realized belonged to the blonde man who had taken a defensive position between Castron and the woman. "The man is right. Your daughter cannot grow old without a mother. She will need you. You must be there to protect her."

She shook her head in protest. "I know you mean well Deacon but I..."

"No. She needs you Kyia." The man named Deacon closed his eyes and drew in a long slow breath. He swallowed hard much the way a warrior preparing for an intense battle might do. He muttered a prayer to the Creator under his breath which Marcus pretended not to hear. And then Deacon said the last thing that Marcus had expected to hear from the man. "I will accept the burden of the bark skin mark from Kyia's babe."

No one dared speak. Not one of them knew what to say. Nor did they understand what had just happened. The man called Deacon was not family to Kyia and the babe. He was not father to the child or husband to the woman. Yet he'd agreed to die for the babe. It made little sense even to Marcus. He was a stranger who'd been willing to die for the small baby. But he'd been willing to die for the babe because he did not want her to grow up without her mother as he'd been forced to do, and because he cared deeply for the woman named Kyia, a woman who reminded him much of his mother.

The flames danced in the braziers upon the wall. The wind howled outside the windows. Snowflakes crept in around the ill-fitting edges of the shutters over the man's windows as the vines snaked their way along the ceiling like a slithering serpent. But inside the house no one dared speak or move. They lingered in agonizing silence, awaiting the merciful moment when someone would break the silence. But each of them was too afraid to be the one to break it.

Fittingly it was Kyia who found her words first. Her face was contorted into a dumfounded stare of confusion. Marcus was afraid that his face probably looked much the same as hers, only with the occasional grimace of pain and fatigue upon his. He watched as the woman reached out a slender hand and placed it gently on the man's arm. "Deacon... Why? Why would you offer this? She isn't your burden to bear."

The blonde man forced a smile, trying to hide his own growing fears and doubts. "You know why. You've always known. Since we were kids playing in the forest, you've known. You were always just afraid to admit to yourself that you knew. Because you didn't want to hurt me."

Tears came streaming down Kyia's face as she looked at the blonde man before her. "I was never worthy of your love Deacon."

Deacon smiled. "No. You were the only one worthy of it."

She shook her head quickly. "I can't let you do this," she said with a quivering lip and trembling voice. "I can't let you trade your life for hers."

"Kyia," Deacon said softly. He took her hand in his own and allowed a small smile to part his thin lips. "If you have any love for me in your heart, any at all... then let me do this. Let me give my life for your daughter. I've never done anything good in my life. Let me do this. Don't take this away from me."

Marcus remained silent. He watched the unfolding scene before him and a pang of guilt tugged at his heart. It should've been him offering his life for the young girl. It should not have fallen to this man to give his life for the babe. It should've been him. The man who had loved her since they were children should not have had to give his life to prove his love for her. He should've been allowed to live and help Kyia raise her daughter. It wasn't right. It wasn't fair.

Kyia was sobbing softly into the man's chest now as he whispered words to her which Marcus could not hear. He did not care that he could not hear them. For the words were not meant for his ears. They were meant for Kyia's ears alone. Words spoken from the man who had loved her since he was a child.

Eventually, she gave the man a nod. With a smile, he gently pushed her away from him and said "Marcus. I am ready to do this ritual if you are as well."

The man felt numb. Everything that had happened was not how he'd foreseen it. It was not how he'd expected this night to go and he wasn't sure how he felt about it. Kyia and her babe would be alright if the ritual worked. That brought him some semblance of happiness. But he'd not intended for an innocent man to lay down his life to save their own. He'd intended for his life to be the one that was ended. His life was not worth more than this man's.

But there was no talking the man out of it. He'd decided to give his life out of love. What greater love was there than to lay down your own life for another? If he stopped this man then he was denying the man the chance to prove how great a love he had for Kyia. And no matter how much he disagreed with this, how much he felt he should've been the one to die this night, he could not rob the man of that. All Marcus could do now was accept that the man's sacrifice was born of greater love than Marcus had ever felt in all his days.

"I'm ready," Marcus managed to say. His words were heavy with guilt. He drew the small dagger at his waist and held it aloft. "Bring the babe and stand before me."

Beads of sweat formed on his brow as Deacon moved closer to him, the baby clutched tightly against his chest. Out of the corner of his eye, Marcus could see the commander watching the events unfolding with cautious eyes that were opened to only narrow slits.

"You'll repeat after me," Marcus instructed the man. Deacon nodded. Marcus cautiously took the young girl's arm and raked the tip of his dagger across the bark skin patch upon her flesh. She did not seem to feel pain as he did it and he was thankful for that. He squeezed her arm gently and a strange liquid akin to some mixture of amber sap and crimson red blood began to ooze from the barked skin. Deacon offered him his arm and Marcus tentatively cut the man's flesh open.

As soon as Marcus saw blood beginning to seep up from the wound in the man's arm, he continued. "By the Old Gods of these lands and the New Ones that replaced them. By the merciful Creator who dwells in the sky. By the earth and sky and all creatures who inhabit them. I, Deacon, do swear upon my blood which is pure to share the burden placed upon this child willingly. This oath I do swear and in doing so, embrace this curse as my own."

Deacon hesitantly repeated the words, stumbling over them as he spoke with a trembling and weak voice which carried no strength at all. It was the voice of a scared man and it made Marcus feel pity. He helped Deacon as best as he could, uttering the words only loud enough for him to hear. While helping the man speak the words, he held the girl's arm so that the strange sap leaking from the bark could fall upon the open wound on Deacon's arm.

As soon as Deacon finished speaking the final word, the fires in the braziers flickered out, plunging the room into complete darkness. There was a yelp of panic and then the sound of the door being ripped open and slamming shut. A moment later, the torches and braziers relit themselves, burning as fiercely and brightly as they had been before they'd been extinguished. The two knights seemed undisturbed by the strange occurrence. Marcus knew such a thing was bound to happen. But Kyia and Deacon looked disturbed, their eyes wide with fear and surprise.

"So now what?" Deacon asked. Marcus nearly chuckled as he watched the blonde man's eyes frantically looking all around the rafters of his home. It was almost as if he expected to see some looming specter swinging from the wooden joists, a wraith which had caused the lights to flicker out. Kyia was clinging to his arm, pressing cloth against the wound in his skin while also checking her daughter's arm.

"All we can do is wait and see what happens," Marcus grumbled, straining to keep his weary and exhausted eyes open. He glanced down at his bloodied leg and saw that the cloth bandage, once as white as the snow falling outside, was strained red with blood and was still growing ever wetter. "Go to sleep. When the morning comes..." Marcus hesitated, unable to bring himself to say that if the ritual was successful the morning would bring Deacon's death. "When the morning comes we'll know if it worked." It was the best he could think to say. And the others must have accepted his words too. For Kyia and Deacon turned and made their way towards the man's bed.

"Marcus, you should come with us," he heard Piers say from somewhere behind him. When he turned, he saw the two knights had reunited and were standing near the door. The apothecary was already gone, having fled in terror when the lights went out in the hut. "Your leg needs tending to or else..."

"I'm not going anywhere," Marcus told the sword master. His eyes found their way to the commander and though he could not be sure he suspected there was a hint of admiration in those old and weary eyes. "If something should happen, this is my doing. I'll handle it."

"But your leg..."

"I will not come with you," he answered. He turned to look at Kyia and Deacon as the two of them crawled onto his bed. They both looked exhausted and he suspected that sleep would soon overcome both of them. The little girl lay peacefully on the cot between the two of them. "I need to be here."

Piers looked ready to protest. But when the commander put his large, calloused hand upon the sword master's shoulder, he fell silent. Marcus watched as Piers trudged towards the door silently, occasionally casting glances over his shoulder towards Marcus' wounded leg. The man was right to worry. He'd packed it with snow, hoping the cold would congeal the blood and stop the bleeding. But the gash was too deep for such a thing to work. Marcus knew that. But he'd thrown his future away to save this babe. He was going to see it through to the end.

Once Piers had exited the home, disappearing amongst the darkness and fierce driving snow outside, Castron grunted to draw Marcus' attention. "Here," the old man said as he offered him a small glass vial from the pouch around his waist. "It's a medicine that we use to numb pain. Use it for your leg if you'd like. Or give it to the one who bears the bark skin mark come the morning. Make their death a painless ordeal. Makes no difference to me." Marcus limped to the old man and took the vial from his grasp. "I do not agree with what you've done here today. You risk the lives of many to save one babe. It is not the way of the knights. But I admire your resolve boy. And for your sake and the sake of the babe... I hope that this works."

"Too bad you have to hang me for treason in the morning or that might have actually seemed like a compliment," Marcus said. The words escaped his mouth before he'd even taken a moment to contemplate them. For a moment, terror gripped his throat. He shouldn't have said that to the old man he'd wronged this day.

But to his relief the commander smirked. "Worry about surviving the night first. Then we can discuss that matter." Castron patted him on the shoulder with a heavy hand which nearly sent him toppling to the floor. And then the old man disappeared into the night.

The room was silent once more, save for the sound of the soft breathing of Kyia and Deacon as they lay sleeping in the bed. Marcus limped to the nearest wall he could find and slumped back against it. He allowed himself to slip down the wall until he was sitting on the floor. The pain in his leg was growing more intense with each passing minute. It throbbed and burned. When he moved, pain shot up his leg faster than a bolt loosed by a crossbow.

But he took the pain. Not because the pain made him feel alive in that moment or served as a reminder that he'd faced one of the most dangerous beasts in all the lands and lived. It wasn't even because the pain reminded him why he had endured all this, how he'd risked his life to save the life of a young babe. He took the pain because it was the only thing he could do to keep from falling asleep.

His heavy eyelids did not seem to feel so heavy and did not threaten to clasp closed on him when he pressed his hand against the wound. The pain was beyond his ability to describe. But he felt like dying could not be this painful. Nor could being stabbed by a thousand daggers which burned as hot as the sun.

The night dragged by painfully slow. Marcus had no idea if it merely seemed that way to him because he was seemingly constantly jabbing his own thumb against the bloodied cloth and choking back yelps of pain every time that his eyelids began to feel heavy.

He sat and listened to the howl of the wind outside. He watched more of the vines crept across the opening to the window and snaked its way into the hut, creeping across the rafters supporting the ceiling. He felt snowflakes landing on his head as they were blown through the gaps in the vines covering the window. And whenever he felt like sleep would overcome him, he pressed his hand against the gash in his leg and bit back a yelp of pain.

After the longest night of his life, Marcus was beyond relieved when he heard a roar carry on the sky. It was the roar of the dragon which ushered the rising sun across the sky each morning and awoke the world. He wasn't sure how he'd done it. But somehow, he'd survived the night without falling asleep, passing out from the pain or dying. A feat he would have celebrated if he was not preparing to kill a man or a baby.

Deacon began to stir in the bed across from him. Marcus watched as he rose from the bed and began to limp across the room to where Marcus lay in a growing pool of his own blood. As Deacon approached, his finger lay upon his arm, right at the point where Marcus' blade had cut flesh in the night. "Marcus, look," Deacon whispered as he flashed his arm. If Marcus would've had more strength, he would've smiled. For upon the man's flesh, growing where his blood had been spilled, was the gray-brown bark.

"Your leg," Marcus croaked. "You did not limp last night, did you?"

Deacon shook his head and pressed his hand against the back of his leg. He nearly yelped in pain and immediately pulled the leg of his trousers up and Marcus saw that the skin upon the back of his leg was missing. A lump formed in his throat when he saw it. That was the spot where he'd stabbed the beast with the axe the night before. That wound was caused by his doing. "Does this mean that it worked?" he asked as he touched the wound again and recoiled in pain.

"Yes," Marcus whispered back, though he'd not intended his words to come out as a whisper. His voice was small and growing smaller with each passing moment. His face was pale white and clammy. A sheen of sweat glistened upon his brow. He shivered in the cold even though his skin felt like it was alight with fire.

Deacon looked back at the bed, at the still sleeping forms of Kyia and her daughter. "Can you do it now? Before she wakes... I don't want her to see it happen."

Marcus mustered the strength to nod his head and handed the vial of strange liquid to the man. "Drink this. It'll numb the pain. You won't feel anything."

Deacon took the vial and drank it in one gulp. His sour face told Marcus it must've tasted terrible. But it was better to drink something sour than suffer the pain. "Where will you do it?"

"Heart," Marcus croaked weakly as his hand clasped around the hilt of his sword. With some degree of difficulty he managed to draw the blade. His strength was fading faster than his resolve. Deacon was a good man who did not deserve any of this. He didn't deserve to die like this. It should've been Marcus.

"Fitting, isn't it?" Deacon asked as he flashed one final look at Kyia. A smile parted his thin lips. "T'was my heart which put me in this situation. Only fitting that my heart is where it ends."

"I'm sorry," Marcus whispered in his ever shrinking voice.

"Don't be," Deacon said in a mock showing of bravery, though there was only sorrow and fear as he prepared to confront his death. "I've made my choice... Kyia and her daughter will grow old. That is how it must be." He took one last deep breath. "It is time."

Marcus waited for the man's eyes to close. Once they were closed, he struck. Marcus' strength was failing quickly. But on that morning he had strength enough to deliver a fatal thrust to the man called Deacon's heart. He did not remember if the man cried out in pain or if the man had even reacted to his thrust at all. The only thing Marcus remembered of that morning was the way he'd felt as he was driving his sword through the man's heart, the frustration and anger and regret and relief that washed over him as the sword bit through the man's chest. Marcus remembered pulling the blade free, looking at the blood of a good man dancing upon his blade.

And then there was blackness.

CHAPTER 8

As Marcus sat in the saddle of his faithful mare, he could hardly believe how much everything seemed to have changed in the days since he'd ended the Lesnik's reign of terror.

After he'd delivered the fatal blow to Deacon and ended the life of the one afflicted with the bark skin mark, Marcus had collapsed from blood loss and nearly died. Kyia had awakened shortly afterwards and managed to get Piers and Castron back to the home in time to save his life. The girl claimed it to be luck. Marcus hadn't agreed. There was no such thing as luck. Especially not in Elesia. It wasn't the unlucky who died in Elesia. It was the weak.

It had taken him three days to awaken from the ordeal. But when he'd awakened, his body was mending itself far faster than should've been possible. The gash on his arm had nearly completely healed and the wound to his leg, which should've seen him limping for weeks, no longer caused him pain. Castron had warned that if he decided to walk upon it so soon after the stitching, he'd rip the wound open again. But on the fourth day, he'd walked to see the burning of Deacon's body and the leg had held up fine to everyone's disbelief.

The chieftain, upon learning of what had transpired the night when the Lesnik's reign of terror was ended, had declared Deacon a hero amongst the people. Castron had told Marcus and Kyia that he'd had no hand in such a thing happening. But Marcus could see the bruising upon the chieftain's cheeks and the small cuts upon the old commander's knuckles clear as day.

The commander had decided that they would not leave the village until the snow had begun to melt as he'd not make the horses trudge up snow covered hills if he did not have to. While he and Piers had spent much of their free time trying to train the town guard and helping to cut away the vines that had tried to reclaim the village, Marcus spent most of his time recovering in Kyia's hut. The woman had grown quite fond of him. And truthfully, Marcus was rather fond of her as well.

But he knew that what they had was a fleeting thing. He'd have loved to have stayed in that village with her and her daughter, to have grown old with Kyia, have children of his own that he could teach to fight and help the people survive in the dark and treacherous woods. But that was not his place. It was no longer the path of life which he had been put upon. The path which he had to travel would not allow him such a simple life. He would either become a knight or be punished for what he'd done in this village. That was his path, whether he liked it or not.

As soon as the snow melted, the three of them would return to the fortress and Marcus would either be initiated into their rank or exiled into the far north to never return to Elesia again. Or he'd be put to death. So Marcus made the best of the time that he had with her. They told stories of their childhood. They drank and ate and celebrated those who had died at the hands of the Lesnik. They honored Deacon and Kyia's husband. And when his leg began to feel better, Marcus even taught the woman how to swing a sword. She hadn't been good at first. But she learned quickly.

They were joyful days which reminded Marcus of the youth which had been stolen from him when his mother had been killed and his father had sent him off to train with the Knights of the King. They were days filled with love and happiness that he feared he would never get to experience. Days that he knew would end. But he wished they would not.

On the eleventh morning, they did.

The air was cold that morning as the three of them tugged the reins of their horses and began to canter out of town, climbing the hillside which they'd raced down two weeks ago. As the horses slowly wound their way up the hill, Marcus found himself unable to stop casting fleeting glances back at the village below them. He'd not even reached the crest of the hill and already he longed to go back and hug Kyia one last time, to kiss her once more and promise he'd return even though he knew it was a lie.

She'd wanted to say goodbye to him this morning as he'd left. He hadn't let her. He didn't want her to say goodbye because every person he'd ever said those words to he hadn't seen again. So instead, she'd told him something that he hoped he'd remember until the end of his days. She'd looked at him lovingly as she said, "Whenever there is a meeting, a parting must always follow. There is no way we can stop such things from happening. But we can be the ones who decide how long that parting must last."

The words had struck something within him. Those were the words that he wished to be her last words to him. So Marcus had kissed Kyia and left without another word.

But now, as he galloped along, he wished he'd have told her something. Anything at all was surely better than the silence he'd left her with. He hoped she knew how much he cared for her. He hoped she knew the love he would always carry in his heart for her and her daughter.

When the horses finally reached the crest of the hill, Marcus looked down on the valley one last time. He took a long, lingering look. His eyes immediately found their way to Kyia's home as smoke billowed out of the chimney top. They lingered there for a long while before the man muttered weakly, "Goodbye Kyia." Then, Marcus drew the reins of the horse back and followed after the knights.

The three of them rode for a long while in silence. There was much that needed to be discussed. Yet none of them seemed willing to speak of it. Their quest was not one that any of them were particularly proud of. Each man had done something that would not be looked kindly upon by time if all were to know of what transpired. Between Piers committing treason, Castron nearly killing a baby instead of finding another solution, and Marcus attacking the commander, the quest had been full of missteps and poor decisions. If not for Marcus' stubbornness and unwavering courage, the quest may have ended in tragedy.

So the three men had agreed that what transpired in the village would remain between them, a secret which all three would take to their graves. And that was to be the end of it. Yet as they rode along Marcus couldn't help but feel that there was something which still needed to be said, a question which he needed to ask and the commander needed to answer. "Castron," he said as he rode his horse alongside the old man.

Castron turned to look at him and raised his white eyebrow in intrigue. "Something you need boy?"

"When we return to the fortress... What happens to me?" Marcus asked rather timidly. He hated asking the old man a question such as this one. He knew what the answer should have been. He should've been hanged or exiled for attacking the commander of their order. There should be no place for him amongst their ranks. Still, he felt he needed to hear the words come out of the old man's mouth before he decided what fate should await him.

"I think it's rather obvious, isn't it?" The old man ran a hand through his white beard. "You disobeyed a direct order. You attacked me. You held me at sword point. Stole the bestiary from my saddlebags. Foolishly rode out into the forest at night to kill a beast which is known to be un-killable. And saved the lives of a baby and the townspeople of Dunwall." The old commander paused for a moment to allow his words to sink in. "You're a great many things boy. You're rash and insubordinate. You're stubborn and bullheaded, courageous and clever. And foolishly brave and willing to fight anyone for what you think is right. Worst of all, you're unwilling to sacrifice one to save many." The commander paused again. "You're a knight, Marcus of Kildwin."

The words felt so surreal when he heard them, Marcus was nearly convinced that he must have been dreaming. After everything that had happened, everything that he had done, the commander had still seen fit to make him a knight. He wasn't sure he'd ever understand why it had happened. But in the moment, he didn't care. He was a Knight of the King. That was all that mattered to him.

"But promise me one thing," the old man continued quickly. "Promise me that you will always do what you think is right. That you will always fight for the right thing. Do not worry about being a perfect warrior or the perfect soldier. But promise me that so long as you serve underneath me you will always be a good man. The same man who was unwilling to kill a single baby to save an entire village. We're taught to sacrifice the few for the many. And you refuse such a thing. I admire that. So don't change who you are."

"I won't," Marcus said with a nod. The old man smiled a toothy grin, one which he did not seek to hide. So Marcus figured now was as good a time as any to tell the commander what he needed to tell him. "So... Should I call you Commander Castron now or...?"

"You may call me Castron. Or Commander Castron if you wish to be formal."

"Right. Commander Castron, you sent me on a quest to kill the monster which was plaguing the village of Dunwall. I wish to report that I failed to kill the Lesnik of Dunwall," Marcus said, half in jest. "I tried. Didn't work."

"You don't say," the commander replied dryly, the smile still separating his face.

"I'm terribly broken up over it. Probably cry myself to sleep tonight because of it."

Castron nodded. "I suppose I should thank you for informing me of your failure."

"And I feel that I must also inform you that if I ever seen

another Lesnik in all my days, I'm going to mind my own fuckin' business and walk the other way."

"You're a Knight of the King now Marcus. We can't do that."

Marcus grumbled and shook his head. "I know. I hate that about us."

The commander laughed and rode his horse onwards to lead them back to the fortress. Marcus allowed himself to smile as the three knights continued riding along the dirt trails which led through the forest. Marcus could hardly believe that he'd become a Knight of the King after all that had happened. But it was as a wise woman had once told him. What happened was meant to happen, which was an expression of faith in the nature of the Creator and the world which they inhabited. His quest to become a Knight of the King was meant to happen that way. If it'd have happened any other way, he wouldn't have become a knight.

All around him, Marcus could hear the sounds of deer and elk and other creatures calling out to one another. He could hear birds singing heavenly choruses and frogs chirping deep amidst the trees. All the sounds he'd longed to hear on his ride into the village of Dunwall greeted his ears as he rode away.

The forests were alive with the sounds of the animals that made the trees their home. That was the way it ought to be.

The smile upon Marcus' face grew even bigger. This was the way the world was supposed to be.

And because of him, it was.

ABOUT THE AUTHOR

Mike D. Martin is an author of fantasy novels. A lifelong native of Cuyahoga Falls, Ohio, he graduated from the University of Akron with a degree in Political Science/Criminal Justice and was on his way to earning a second degree in Respiratory Therapy before he decided to pursue a career in writing. He credits both *The Lord of the Rings* and *The Legend of Zelda* series as the fantasy stories which inspired him to create his own fantasy books. *The Terror of Dunwall* is the first book in *The Knight from Kildwin* series. He is also the author of *The Elesian Tales Saga* series.

www.ingramcontent.com/pod-product-compliance
Lightning Source LLC
Chambersburg PA
CBHW061222210726

48294CB00006B/1940